WHAT CORAL WANTS

WHAT CORAL WANTS

TERA LYNN CHILDS

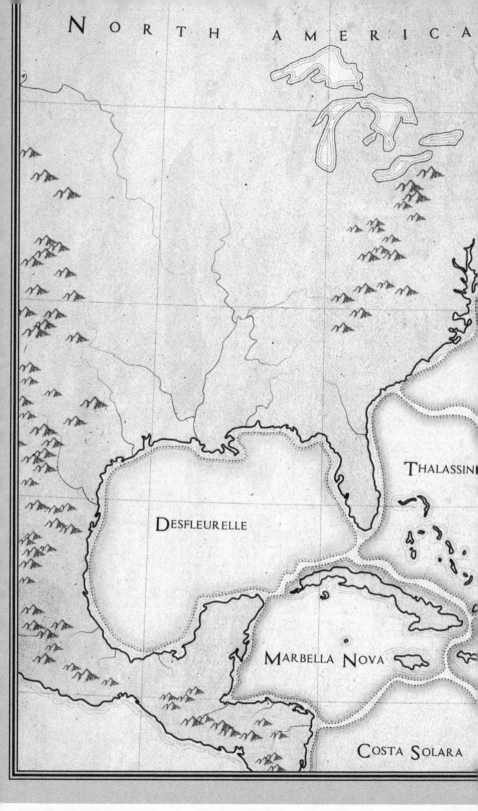

ROSMARUS

NEPHROPIDA

GONUM

THE
TRICONUM
VORTEX

CENTRAL ATLANTIC

MER KINGDOMS
OF THE WESTERN ATLANTIC

PORA

ANTILLENES

ONE

Friday afternoon

FORTY-SEVEN DAYS.

It's been forty-seven days since I last saw Zak Marlin.

That probably doesn't seem like a long time. Less than two months, right? But before the day he swam off for orientation at University of the Western Atlantic at Desfleurelle, I saw him almost every single day for four straight years. Forty-seven days feels like a lifetime.

I've told myself to stop counting. Begged myself even.

Come on, Coral. Get your act together. Get over him.

Wasn't four years of loving from afar enough? Haven't I earned a break from thinking about him every waking moment?

Okay, not *every* waking moment. I have good grades, am involved in several extracurriculars, and help out in my family's pearl business when they need me.

But whenever I have a free moment, my mind drifts to him.

Where is he right now?

What's he doing?

Is he enjoying college?

Has he made new friends?

Does he get homesick?

I have no right to ponder these questions. At least no more right than anyone else at Queen Sirenia Academy. He's not technically anything special to me. QSA's star seaball player. My best friend's older brother. Another mergirl's boyfriend.

We're friends, I guess, but nothing more. Never more.

You'd think I would have learned my lesson by now.

Big crushes die hard.

And believe me, I've tried to kill it.

Why am I telling you all of this right up front? We just met, and here I am spilling my deepest, darkest secret. (Seriously, don't tell anyone. No one, not even my best friend knows. Because, you know, sister of said crush and all.)

Anyway, I'm telling you this because I want you to understand the full impact of what I feel when I float out of school on an ordinary afternoon and swim straight into Zak Marlin's chest.

I'm not looking where I'm going. In a rush to get home, I speed around a corner and *BLAM!* Crush crash.

I know immediately that it's him. In the same way a mermom knows her guppy's cry from an ocean away. The instant my cheek connects with his t-shirt-covered shoulder, I know.

I want to laugh and cry at the same time.

His hands come up to catch me—or maybe to push me away since I, you know, just smashed into him. The heat from his palms sends a shiver all the way to the tip of my tailfin.

In a flash, I re-memorize everything about his face. The way his dark gold brows frown low over his kelp-green eyes. The way his curls wave a little longer because he hasn't gotten a haircut since he left. The way his cheeks flush dusky pink—possibly because he just had a near-death collision with a speedy mergirl.

I take it all in because I've been in withdrawal for forty-seven days and I don't know why he's here or how long he's staying.

A mergirl has to look her fill while she can.

"Are you all—" Zak's concerned expression morphs into a grin. "Coral!"

Keep it together.

As quick as a mackerel evading a shark, I shove the lovesick version of myself down deep inside and replace it with the fun-loving-little-sister's-best-friend character I've been playing for years. I've had so much practice playing this role that you'd think I'd start to believe it myself.

Not a chance.

The rest of the mer world might be clueless, but my heart sees through the facade.

"Guilty," I reply with a perilously fake grin. "I didn't know you were coming home."

The blush in his cheeks deepens.

"I haven't told anyone. It's a surprise."

"Does your family know?"

He shakes his head. "I needed to stop by school first."

My heart dances at the thought that *I* know this secret, that I'm the first merperson to know that he's home.

"What's the surprise?" I ask.

He releases my arms and shoves a hand through his curls.

As chilly seawater rushes in where his hands had been, I shiver again—in a less thrilling way this time.

If I was at all capable of playing it cool, at this point I would think something smooth like, *I totally forgot he was still holding them.* But, let's be honest, I have been acutely and painfully aware of every single instant of contact.

"Coach asked me to come," he says. "He wants me to give a speech at the Give Back Game."

I don't miss the tiny tremor in his voice.

Despite his perfection in nearly every possible way, Zak has always been nervous about speaking in front of crowds. A public speaker he is not. He once faked sick to get out of presenting his science fair project.

The Give Back Game is about as much *public* as you can get.

Even though the team's record has been awful since losing Zak, the crowd at this game—pretty much the most popular event of QSA's annual Give Back Week— will be huge. Current students, faculty, alumni, and all their families will come out to support the team and donate to the school's charitable foundation. The stands will be full.

No wonder Zak sounds nervous.

I try to sound as positive as possible. "Wow, that's great!"

Maybe it's unkind of me, but seeing this tiny weakness in him—this chip in the otherwise flawlessness of the great Zak Marlin—only makes me love him more. It makes him seem more…*real*.

"So you'll be home all Give Back Week?" I ask, partly to distract him from the thought of public speaking, but mostly because I want—no, I *need*—to know.

Even though we're technically friends, we're not *friends* friends. It's not like we've been exchanging message bubbles since he went away. Or that I could ask Zanzie about him without raising her suspicions. I've been in a Zak-related blackout.

"Yep, all week," he says. "We're on mid-semester break at school."

Did my heart do a little dance earlier? Now it's breaking into a complete flash mob routine. An entire week of him? My Zak-starved brain is ecstatic.

The only thing that dampens my joy is the little shadow that comes over his eyes. No one else would see it, but—like I said—I'm a little obsessed with the details when it comes to Zak. So I notice.

It's not the same as his nerves about public speaking, either. It's something different.

"What?" I float ever-so-slightly closer. "What's wrong?"

"Nothing." He shakes his head, like he doesn't want to discuss it. "It's just…"

But maybe he does.

I hold my breath.

He rubs his hand over his face. "Angel and I broke up."

"What?!"

Did I scream that out loud?

It feels like a tsunami just crashed into me and knocked the breath out of my lungs. Zak? Angel? Break-up? After *two years*?! I can't compute this news.

"I mean—" I clench my hands into fists to keep from clapping in giddy joy. Bad form, that. "I thought you guys were practically engaged."

The shadow in his eyes darkens a little. He closes them for a second, and when he opens them the shadow is gone. His mouth quirks to one side in a self-effacing grin that is #2 on my list of favorite Zak smiles.

I bite my lip to keep from grinning back like a fool.

"Not quite," he says. "But I think everyone was expecting that. I guess Angel didn't think the long-distance thing could work."

All the water rushes back into my lungs at once.

It takes every last drop of my willpower not to shout, *SHE broke up with YOU!?!!!* Who in their right mind would dump Zak Marlin?

Angel must be insane.

Being the very good friend that I am—and not at all the girl who has been desperately in love with him for years and sees her first real chance at everlasting happiness finally within her reach—I nod sympathetically. I deserve a friend-ship award.

"I'm sorry," I say, trying to make sure my expression matches my solemn words and not my exuberant thoughts. "Getting dumped sucks."

He winces.

Maybe I shouldn't have put it that way.

I don't have much—or, you know, any—experience in dumpdom. With my emotions romantically engaged elsewhere, I haven't exactly been participating in the QSA dating pool. But I can imagine getting dumped is a sore subject.

"My mom definitely thinks it sucks," he says. "She won't let it go."

"What do you mean?"

Mrs. Marlin is like my second mom. Because my mom has to work so much, sometimes taking weeks-long pearl-hunting trips around the seven seas, I've spent a lot of dinners over the last few years sitting across the Marlin table from Zak.

"Mom's convinced that Angel will change her mind," he explains. "That we'll be back together before winter break so we can go to the dance together."

And just like that, my growing balloon of hope pops like a pufferfish who doesn't know when to stop puffing.

Mrs. Marlin is right. A relationship like the one between Zak and Angeleria Hind doesn't end just because someone goes off to college. They've been virtually inseparable since they first started going out two years ago. While other teen relationships were on and off again—and again and again—Zak and Angel (or Zangel, as everyone at school calls them) were immune.

I don't know what Angel was thinking, but chances are she'll change her mind.

As depressing as that is, I'm glad I realized it now. It

would only get more painful the longer I let myself believe I might finally have a chance.

Coming back down to the seafloor before you float too high is easier than crashing back into the sea after soaring too close to the sun.

"Maybe your mom is right," I suggest.

He huffs out an awkward laugh.

"Not you, too," he says. "Ever since I told her, it's like all she can do is imagine the little blond grandguppies she won't be getting. She's relentless."

"When you put it that way…"

I think his mom is right about an inevitable Zangel reunion, but I also think that my loyalty is to Zak. Surely I can protect my heart *and* be supportive at the same time.

I give him a sympathetic smile. "As if you can do anything to change Angel's mind."

"Try telling my mom that."

There's that quirk-smile I love.

"That's why I didn't tell her I was coming home for Give Back Week. When she finds out, she'll be nonstop."

He presses his hands to his face, like he can't stand the thought.

"You know what she said in her last bubble message?" he asks, dropping his hands away. He doesn't wait for a response. "That I should pretend to see someone to make Angel jealous."

"You don't think it would work?" I ask.

It would definitely make *me* jealous.

He doesn't hesitate. "No."

"I bet it would work," I say with a laugh, "on your mom."

He frowns in confusion, wondering what I'm talking about.

"Pretending to date someone," I explain. "It might get your mom off you back."

And I bet it *would* make Angel jealous.

I beat myself up for making the suggestion as I watch a series of emotions play across Zak's face. Confusion into understanding into consideration into—*Oh no.*

He flashes #4 on my list of favorite smiles. The big, broad one that means he's got everything figured out.

The instant I see it, I know I'm in trouble. I wish I could reach out and grab my words back.

If only speech bubbles worked like message bubbles.

"You know..." He draws the words out, like he's trying to coast his way into the sentence.

My stomach plummets. I find myself instinctively inching back.

"That's not a bad idea." He floats forward, closing the gap I just made. "What if we—"

No, no, no. This has to be the worst idea ever.

If I were any kind of romantically savvy, you might think I knew what I was doing when I suggested it. You might think it was some devious master plan. Convince Zak to fake date me—for his own good, of course—with the hope that the fake would fade away and we would just end up dating.

I wish I were that clever.

But I know me. And I know Zak and Angel. There is no

way this scenario ends with anything but me crying myself into oblivion.

"Come on," Zak argues. "My mom loves you. She'll lay off the Angel stuff if she thinks we're together."

"I know, but—"

"Plus, it's Give Back Week. We could go to everything together. I kinda hate the idea of going to all that stuff alone."

I feel myself shaking my head.

I also feel myself considering the idea. Give Back Week is full of activities—the carnival, the big game, the talent show. How much fun would it be to go to those events with Zak?

And to go in the guise of boyfriend and girlfriend?

It would be the culmination of my every high school dream. Don't I deserve that?

"It would be a blast. No drama." He gestures in the water between us. "Just friends hanging out and having a good time. Like always."

Like always.

The words echo in my mind like a shout into the Marianas Trench. *Like always. Like always. Like always.*

That's when I know I can't do this. Because as much as I want to spend every possible second with Zak while he's home, I know that the emotional cost will be too high.

It wouldn't be real. It would only be a matter of time before it comes to an end. Zak and Angel will be together again before he swims back to college, and I'll be left even more heartbroken than before.

Which is why, instead of giving in to the desperate

desire to agree, I say, "Hahaha, I could never pretend to be your girlfriend. It would be too...weird."

As if the thought had never, ever, in a million tiny ways crossed my mind.

"You're probably right. Dumb idea." His mouth kicks up to one side as he shrugs it off. "Will you be at dinner Sunday night?"

I smile, only partly relieved that this whole horrible idea is over. Zak let that go way too easily. Maybe the thought of pretending to be my boyfriend actually was too weird for him.

If that doesn't do wonders for my self-esteem, I don't know what does.

Brushing off the ego-bruise, I answer enthusiastically, "Wouldn't miss it."

Saying no was the right decision. I know that.

But as we swim our separate ways, I can't help wondering what it would have been like to pretend to be Zak's girlfriend for a week. Did I dismiss the idea too quickly? Yes, it would hurt. But so does seeing him with Angel. Maybe the price would have been worth it?

I guess now I'll never know.

TWO

Sunday night

THE MARLIN HOUSE is just as much my home as the one I share with my mom and brother. I've lost count of how many family dinners I've eaten, how many sleepovers Zanzia and I have had, how many times Mrs. Marlin has had to sign a consent form because Mom was halfway around the world at a pearl convention.

I usually swim right in without even knocking.

Not tonight. As I float outside the familiar blue door, my heart thunders like I'm about to have an audience with King Whelk. I don't think I've ever felt this nervous before.

It's not *only* because I know Zak is inside. Until two months ago, almost every Marlin family dinner I was part of included him. Even when he started dating Angel, Sunday dinners were non-negotiable.

The last several without him felt like putting together a

puzzle with a missing piece. You can still see the picture, but it's just not complete.

Now that he's back, everything should feel right again.

But it's the first time in ages that Zak is single. It's like that lost puzzle piece got left out in the sun and now it's a slightly different color than before.

Even though I know he won't be single for long, I don't think I remember how to act around him when he is. Can I pull off appearing to be a normal mergirl?

I touch my hair, the thick, dark curls twisted up into a topknot. I pull at the hem of my tankini top, a deep peachy-pink that matches the darkest shade of scales on my tailfin.

Normally a bare-faced girl, tonight I actually broke out the lip gloss. Which will probably end up smeared all over the place before the night is over because I can't be trusted not to touch my face.

I'm just swiping the back of my hand across my mouth to remove the soon-to-be-wayward gloss when the door flies open.

"Coral!!!" Zanzia squeals.

In an instant, my best friend is yanking me into a fierce hug.

"Your hair," I say.

When I last saw Zanzie—right before I ran into Zak outside of school two days ago—her hair was the same golden shade of blond as his. Sometime between then and now, she conducted one of her famous *experiments*.

"I know!" She releases me and floats back so she can swirl around. "Isn't it everything?"

Instead of that enviable shade of gold, her hair is the brightest, boldest shade of magenta that I have ever seen outside of the anemone superbloom in the eastern sand fields a few years ago.

"It's...*something*."

Zanzie knows I don't mean it as an insult. We might be best friends, but in so many ways we are total opposites. And not just in looks.

I would never be daring enough to color my hair. Certainly not anything so wild and crazy as neon fuchsia.

Zanzia eats daring for breakfast. And lunch, dinner, and midnight snack.

"Oh!" She squeals louder than before. "You don't know!"

Before I can ask what I don't know, she grabs me by the wrist and drags me into the house. With a flick of her tailfin, the front door shuts behind us.

My heart beats harder into my throat. I can guess what she *thinks* I don't know. And boy oh merboy do I already know.

"You'll never guess!" She swims us through the house, toward the kitchen. "Zak is—"

"Home," I finish for her.

As she floats through the kitchen doorway, she spins to face me. "How did you know?"

"I—"

Before I can answer, she whirls back into the kitchen. "You said you didn't tell anyone you were coming home."

Beyond her, I can see Zak getting plates out of the

cupboard. He flashes his sister a gentle smile—#7 on my list.

"I didn't, Z." He glances at me. "I ran into Coral outside the school."

Ran into being the operative phrase. I don't miss that little wink. Neither does my stupid heart.

If I get through this dinner without having a straight up heart attack it will be a miracle. One more wink might just do me in.

"Coral, welcome!" Mrs. Marlin cheers. "Here, put this on the table for me, would you?"

I take the platter laden with tuna burgers—which I, for completely normal, non-stalkery reasons, know is Zak's favorite dish—and float into the dining room. My stomach grumbles. I'd been too nervous about dinner to eat anything today, which means I'm completely starving. I could eat every burger and then some.

Mr. Marlin is already at the table, the current issue of the *Thalassinia Times* held open before him.

There is no doubt where Zanzia gets her overflowing personality. Mrs. Marlin is full of more energy than a school of electric eels, while Mr. Marlin is more…reserved. He's a bookkeeper who spends his days with spreadsheets and expense reports.

Zak is a pretty even mix of the two.

I return to the kitchen to see if I can help more.

"Zanzie, get some of that special strawberry jelly that Coral likes so much," Mrs. Marlin says. "I think there's a jar hiding behind the ginger pickles."

While Zanzia hunts for the jelly jar, Mrs. Marlin dishes

spicy calamari into a large bowl. I float over to the drawer that holds the utensils and grab five sets of seasticks.

"I may have overdone it with the food," Mrs. Marlin says. Her voice takes on a too-sweet-to-be real tone. "Zak, honey…"

A shiver of dread washes down my spine.

Out of the corner of my eye I sense Zak stiffen.

Zanzia whirls around, jar of jelly in hand. "Found it."

Mrs. Marlin adds some spices to the bowl and stirs them into the calamari. She's not even looking at Zak when she asks, "Are you sure you don't want to invite Angel?"

My eyes dart to him.

His cheeks are suddenly a little darker.

"I'm sure," he mutters.

Zanzia leans over to me and whispers, "They broke up."

I don't say that I already know. Partly because I don't want to have to explain the whole conversation Zak and I had outside the school—especially the part about the ridiculous idea that we should pretend to date to get his mom to back off.

But also because Zak looks like he wants a whirlpool to open up above him and suck him up into the sky.

Mrs. Marlin seems unfazed by his response. How can she not see how much her suggestion bothers him?

She hands the calamari to Zak and then shoos the three of us toward the dining room.

In a flurry, everyone rushes to the table. Mrs. Marlin floats at the end opposite where Mr. Marlin is still reading his paper. I take my normal spot next to Zanzia.

"Save me," Zak whispers as he floats over me and sets

the bowl down on the table before swimming around to the other side.

His tone is joking. Like he's making a fake anguished plea for my help. But there is a hint of serious desperation underneath the humor.

"Mr. Marlin!" Mrs. Marlin chastises. "Put that paper away."

"Sorry, dear." He quickly rolls the kelpaper back up and sets it on the table next to his plate. He'll have it back out by the time Mrs. Marlin brings out dessert.

Mrs. Marlin holds out her hands. I take one, and Zak takes the other. Zanzia takes my other hand and closes the circle with her father.

The first time I ate at the Marlin house, this freaked me out. At home, we just dig in as soon as the food is on the table. Even all these years later, it still feels a little weird. But I'm more used to it now.

"Thank Poseidon for this bounty," Mrs. Marlin says, "and for Zak's return."

She beams as Zak gives her an embarrassed smile.

"It's only for a week," he replies.

"A week is better than none." She gives my hand a squeeze and then breaks the circle. "Let's eat."

Food starts passing around the table. I take two tuna burgers off the platter. My stomach grumbles, but I explain to it that it can't have three. That would be too greedy. I promise it an extra helping of everything else instead.

"Everything looks delicious," Mr. Marlin says as he scoops a load of calamari onto his plate.

Mrs. Marlin twitters that it was nothing, but her smile could light up the entire palace.

"It does," I tell her. "I wish I could eat the whole spread myself."

Zak cough-laughs.

His mom ignores him. "You go right ahead, Coral. Eat as much as you like." She flashes a smirk in her son's direction. "Help yourself to Zak's share."

"Whoa-whoa." Zak wraps his arms around his plate, protecting his dinner. "Is this how you treat your favorite son?"

"You're my *only* son," she replies with a straight face.

"Which makes me your favorite."

Mrs. Marlin just shakes her head at Zak's response and goes back to sending platters around the table.

I bite back a laugh. The snappy banter is one of my favorite parts of dinner with the Marlins. Mrs. Marlin may look like a sweet stay-at-home mom, but she can give sass as good as she gets. Even Mr. Marlin throws a zinger every now and then. It's never boring at this table, that's for sure.

My plate is so full I don't think I can fit another spoonful of garlic seabeans. But I'm going to try.

Zanzia takes the kelpberry salad bowl from her dad. "Isn't anyone going to comment on my hair?"

I didn't realize she'd only *just* done it before dinner. This is the big debut. She was probably expecting a big fuss about it.

Instead, Mr. Marlin casually asks, "Oh, have you done something different?"

She tosses a kelpberry at him.

"It's very..." Mrs. Marlin searches for the right word. "Colorful?"

"It's for Give Back Week," Zanzia says.

"Because whoever sold you that color should give back your money?" Zak teases.

Zanzie sticks her tongue out. "It's an homage to this year's theme: *Thalassinia in Bloom*."

"Such a romantic theme." Mrs. Marlin spreads a spoonful of seaweed relish onto her burger bun. "Zak, you should send a bouquet of ruby anemones to Angel."

My eyes dart again to Zak at the mention of his ex. A flash of red brighter than any anemone crawls up his cheeks as he keeps his attention focused on his plate.

"Mom, I told you. We broke up." He pushes a seabean around with a fork. "I'm not sending her flowers."

"Technically, sea anemones are animals," Mr. Marlin says.

Mrs. Marlin sets the spoon back in the relish dish and then hands it to me.

"Angel will come to her senses," she tells Zak. "You don't just throw away all those good years because one of you goes away to university."

I scoop some relish onto my plate and then pass it on to Zanzia.

Across the table, Zak absently stabs at the seabean. He's staring in the general direction of his food, but he clearly isn't seeing anything.

I've never seen him look so miserable. Not even that time he broke his arm in the championship game of the kingdom seaball tournament.

He looks like he just wants to vanish.

This is so the opposite of the Zak I know and love. What happened to his overflowing confidence and ever-present smile? This is not okay.

In that instant, something inside me shifts. Any concern for the safety of my heart floats right out the window. All I can think of is wiping that pain from his eyes.

His hurt is hurting me more.

Which is why I straighten my spine, take a deep breath, and say, "Zak, stop being so shy."

He looks up, his brows furrowed deep over his kelp-green eyes.

"What's that, dear?" Mrs. Marlin asks.

I paste the spunky-little-sister's-best-friend smile on my face and turn to look at her.

"We weren't going to tell anyone." I bat my lashes.

I have never before in my life batted my lashes even one time, but I swear I do. Drastic times call for drastic actions.

"It happened kind of suddenly, but…" I turn to face him. He's looking at me with a mix of hope and panic. Or maybe that's just me projecting. "Zak, you tell them."

He doesn't hesitate. Doesn't even draw a breath before saying, "Coral and I are dating."

He said it. He actually said it. Out loud and everything. Just like it was real.

Which it so totally absolutely is not.

But still. Zak said the words, and my brain can't handle it. My thoughts swirl and there is a buzzing in my ears that might mean I'm having a stroke.

"What?!"

I think only one merperson at the table says that out loud—I can't be too sure because, you know, stroke. They are all thinking it, though. They have to be.

I keep my eyes laser-focused on Zak because if I look around, if I see the shocked expressions on the rest of the Marlin family right now, I might just crumble.

But Zak? Zak looks relieved. And grateful. And *happy*.

That's when I know I made the right decision. Whatever the consequences turn out to be—the most imminent one might be me throwing up all over Mrs. Marlin's beautifully set table—they will be worth it because I put that look on Zak's face. I took away that miserable version of him and brought back the Zak everyone knows and loves.

I am only vaguely aware of anyone else's reactions. Mrs. Marlin says something about how surprised and pleased and *surprised* she is. Mr. Marlin grumbles something about seeing it coming and then picks up his paper. Zanzia just stares in full-blown disbelief.

None of that matters. Not as long as that shadow version of Zak is banished to wherever it came from.

It's not until much later, after the dishes are done and put away and I'm swimming my way home alone—outside of the radiant glow that is Zak's most powerful smile—that the dread resurfaces.

What have I done? What. Have. I. Done?

THREE

Sunday night, later

As I KICK along the well-swum path between the Marlin house and mine, I can't help feeling like I've made a horrible mistake. A horrible, dreadful, lifetime-of-regret mistake.

On the one hand, I get to spend the next week pretending to date Zak, aka the object of my love-from-afar for way-too-long. Shouldn't I be flipping for joy?

But on the other hand…it's not real. We'll be *pretending*. He didn't really ask me out or want me to be his girlfriend. He just wants a shield. Protection against his mom's nagging and probably against the school's pity.

If I were in his fins, I might do the same thing.

It's not like he *knew* about my crush and that he was simultaneously making and breaking my heart. For all he knew, he was just asking a friend for a favor. And what kind of friend wouldn't do that simple favor?

Besides, it might work out for me. Dating Zak might do wonders for my popularity. Not that I've ever cared that much about popularity. But maybe a boost up the social ladder would let me bring more attention to the environmental club.

And I do get to live out my fantasy of dating my crush. Fake dating him is certainly more than I ever expected.

After all, crushes aren't meant to come true. This is as close as I'll ever get.

Which makes it simultaneously wonderful and dangerous.

I swim over the park that separates our neighborhoods. The field of colorful cribinopsis that lines the eastern edge of the park has started to bloom in an autumn-hued rainbow of reds, yellows, and oranges. When I swam this way last week, those colors were nowhere in sight.

It's amazing how much can change in such a short time.

This time next week, Zak will be heading back to school and our fake relationship will be over. How much will have changed by then?

If I'm not careful, pretending to date Zak is *really* going to break my heart.

I've managed to keep my feelings for him under control over the last four years because there's always been a distance between us. An impenetrable wall. Partly the fact that he's my best friend's brother, but also, his unavailability. His relationship with Angel ensured that I never let my hopes float too high.

It would be foolish to let them float into the stratosphere now. Just because Angel broke up with him doesn't mean that they're over.

And this fake relationship just might make her see the error of her ways. A bit of jealousy to hook Angel and reel her back in. If there is one thing guaranteed to make a girl regret dumping her ex, it's seeing him with someone new.

She's going to want him back in no time.

If I don't take steps to protect my heart first, this is going to end badly. I can't let that happen. I value my relationship with the entire Marlin family too much.

I give my tailfin a powerful flick to reverse direction and start swimming back to their house. When I arrive, instead of going to the front door, I head straight for Zak's bedroom window.

Not wanting to be a creepy peeping Tomasina, I float up against the wall and tap lightly on the screen.

"Zak?" I whisper-call.

A moment later, the screen slides open and Zak leans out the window.

"Coral?" He blinks several times. "I thought you were heading home."

Yeah, me too.

"We need to talk," I tell him. "Meet me in the castle."

Without waiting for him to respond, I push off and head into the yard.

Mr. Marlin built the sandcastle years before Zanzie and I even met. It's a rough replica of the Thalassinian royal palace, with just enough room inside for a group of little mergirls to play princess. Or for two teen mergirls to have a place to hide away from the world.

Zanzie and I used to spend hours out here. Daydreaming. Doing homework. Staring up at Zak's window, hoping for the tiniest glimpse of him.

Okay, so that last one was only me.

I float into the sandcastle and down onto the small bench carved into the back wall, mentally composing my thoughts into words.

"Hey there."

Zak fills the entire doorway. His golden hair swirls around him like a liquid halo even as his head almost brushes the top of the opening. His deep violet tailfin looks black in the filtered moonlight.

"I didn't get a chance to thank you. For what you did in there." He gestures over his shoulder, toward the house. "You saved me a lot of grief."

He starts to float into the castle.

I hold up my palm to stop him.

"Rules," I blurt.

In my defense, I don't think I've ever been alone with Zak in an enclosed space. My mind isn't working properly. I only know that he can't get any closer than he already is. I know that's not practical if we're dating—I mean, *fake* dating. But right now, I need to think clearly, and his very presence makes that hard enough.

Zak hesitates, and then continues to float toward me. "Rules?"

"Ground rules," I say, struggling to keep my voice and breathing steady.

I can do this. I have to do this.

"Before this begins—" I gesture at the ever-narrowing

space of water between us. "—we need to lay out the ground rules."

Zak smiles. "Agreed."

And then he floats down next to me on the bench. On the very *small* bench. On the bench that is so small that, in order for us both to fit, our shoulders have to touch.

Just keep breathing, Coral.

I stare straight ahead and focus on my mentally-composed speech.

"First off, and this is the most important rule of all." I want to give him a hard look for good measure, but since I'm trying to avoid any unnecessary contact—eye or otherwise—I keep my gaze trained on the door. "No one can know that this is fake. *No one.* It has to look like a real relationship."

He nods.

"I don't want to be the school joke," I explain. "*Haha, look, Zak Marlin took his little sister's best friend to the Give Back Week Carnival. They have to believe it's real.*"

A tiny little voice in the back of my mind insists that I don't care about being a joke. That I only care about getting to live the fantasy of being Zak's girlfriend as fully as possible, even if it's only for a few days.

I tell that voice to go find a deep, dark hole and swim into it. I have a heart to protect.

"You could never be a joke." Zak absently swirls his tailfin into a figure eight.

He sounds so sincere that I can't help but look up. His green eyes are warm and earnest, and I know in that instant that he would never knowingly hurt me. Knowingly being the operative word. That doesn't mean he couldn't hurt me all the same.

My concern must show on my face because he tries again.

"Everyone will believe that our relationship is real." He holds up three spread fingers in a Sea Scouts salute. "Promise."

I huff out a relieved breath.

"Zanzie may be the actor in the family," he says, "but I can play the doting boyfriend for a week."

"Doting?" I reply with a laugh. "Seriously?"

He puffs out his chest. "I've read Jane Austen."

I swear I fall in love with him a little more. I don't know how that's possible, but I do.

Which in no way helps me protect myself from a broken heart. I have to get this conversation back on track.

"Secondly, if something comes up and either of us needs it to end," I say, "it ends. It's over. Clean break, no discussion."

"Deal," he says.

I don't like how eagerly he agreed to that one. Like he's expecting to want it ended early. Maybe he is. Maybe he thinks it won't take long to make Angel jealous enough to get back together.

Which is exactly why that rule is so important. Whether it's Angel coming to her senses or Zak going back to college, this relationship has an imminent expiration date.

I need to remember that from the start.

"Any other rules?" he asks.

I shake my head. "Nope, just the two."

Fingers, fins, and eyes crossed that those are enough to keep my heart safe.

"I should swim you to school," he suggests. "In the morning."

I make a kind of choking sound. "What?"

"If we're going to make it look real," he says, "then people need to see us together. The more people the better."

The more people the better. My stomach flips over.

He continues, oblivious to the return of my dread. "I'll meet you at your house before school so we can swim over from there."

"Um, yeah, okay," I stammer. "My address is—"

"I know where you live."

He says it like it's no big deal. Like *of course* he knows where I live.

Of course.

A thousand thoughts flash through my mind at once. As far as I know, Zak has never been to my house. Even Zanzia has only been there a few times. I'm not embarrassed by my house or anything, it's just…. Coming to the Marlin house is like floating into a perfect family dream. Always something yummy brewing in the kitchen. Always a full table and lively conversation. I wouldn't trade my mom or brother for anything, but at the Marlins' I get to be part of a different kind of family. I'd almost always rather visit Zanzia there than the other way around.

The idea that Zak knows where I live fills my chest with a big, blooming bubble of joy. Probably glitter-filled.

"Oh. Okay. Great," I tell him. "I'll see you in the morning then."

Only it comes out more like *ohokaygreatillseeyouinthe-morningthen!*

Totally chill.

Zak looks like he's biting back a smile.

Why, Coral, why? Stop acting like such a freak.

Ignoring his amusement, I hold out my hand to shake on it because it feels like the proper thing to do. To seal our deal with a formal gesture.

Zak apparently isn't into formality.

He takes my hand—sending delicious shivers up and down my spine—and then tugs me closer—if that's even possible on this tiny bench—and leans toward me.

In the micro-instant before his lips brush gently against my cheek, I realize what he's about to do and my heart literally explodes. Coral-colored glitter *everywhere.*

My brain processes the sensations in single word flashes.

Soft.

Warm.

Electric.

Perfect.

Then, before I can even fully process what just happened, it's over. Zak is sitting back on his own end of the bench—aka basically on my side, but more upright—and flashing me that Mr. Perfect grin.

"See you in the morning," he says.

He winks, and then pushes off from the bench and swims away, out through the door and across the yard. Presumably back up to his room.

I'm not sure how long I sit there. Five minutes. Five years. Five centuries.

All of eternity wouldn't be enough time for me to recover from that.

Zak. Marlin. KISSED ME!!!!!

Cue the singing lobsters and twirling starfish.

Sure, it was only on the cheek, but technically still a kiss. He touched me with his lips. Even in my deepest fantasies, the only realistic way I ever thought that would happen was if I got bit by a venomous sea snake and he had to suck the venom out or I would die.

I still might die. It's possible to die of joy, right?

I lean back into the rough sand surface of the castle wall, trying to bring my thoughts, my breathing, and my heart rate back under control.

It takes a while.

When I finally feel capable of swimming home, I push up from the bench and follow the path Zak took out of the sandcastle. As I make my way through the Thalassinian suburbs, I'm one-thousand-percent sure I'm blushing almost as much as I'm grinning. Which is to say a *lot*.

The farther I get from the Marlin house, out of the sphere of Zak's influence, the more reality tries to set in.

This whole thing could end badly. Painfully, heartbreakingly badly.

I should be worried about that. I should be having a serious conversation with my heart about what to feel and not feel. I should be treating this as a friendly favor, nothing more.

But I can't stop smiling.

I press my hand to my cheek. Who has time to worry about the future when the present is the stuff of dreams?

For right now, I'm not going to think about it. I'm not going to think about the end. I'm going to focus on the beginning, on the wild and crazy ride that the next few days are going to bring. I'm going to enjoy it while I can.

When it ends, it ends. I just have to hope that my heart will survive when it does.

FOUR

Monday morning

SOME MERFOLK ENJOY MORNINGS. They flop out of bed while it's still dark so they can watch the early morning sunlight turn the midnight waters into a vibrant turquoise blue.

I am *not* one of those merfolk. Sunrises are for suckers. The later I can sleep, the better.

Growing up, Mom (or, if she wasn't home, my brother Riatus) would have to forcibly pull me from my bed in the morning. Once I got to upper school, it got better. I am now capable of rousting myself…eventually.

Some mornings are still a struggle.

When the light reaches in through my window and tickles my nose, I turn away from it, burrowing deeper into my bed.

I was having the most delicious dream. I can't remember what it was about—something about playing seaball in the palace maybe—but it was definitely worth returning to. If only I could lull my brainwaves back into that story.

Not today, apparently.

I desperately want to doze for another fifteen or twenty or ninety minutes, but my brain is ready to pop out of bed and get this day started. Like it has a reason to greet the day instead of diving back into the dream.

It takes me five precious minutes to remember why.

I bolt upright, my covers swirling away from me and toward the corner of my room.

"*Zak!*"

My heart pounds like I've just swum a marathon.

Zak Marlin is going to be at my house—I check the clock on my nightstand—soon! Zak Marlin is coming to swim me to school, and I'm not even fully awake yet.

Don't freak out, Coral. Act like a sane mergirl.

The pep talk doesn't work.

I don't have time to worry about that. I'll just have to push through. And quickly.

Faster than I've ever gotten ready for school before, I race through my morning routine.

Brush my teeth. Brush my hair. Scrub my face. Brush my hair *again* because it got all tangled during my face scrubbing. Decide to attempt a braid to keep my hair from retangling. Give up and just let it do its thing. Change from my sleep shirt into something more appropriate.

That last one is harder than it should be.

What exactly is *appropriate* in this situation? Considering I've never been in anything like this before, I'm swimming blind here.

Plain black tankini? Boring.

Bright pink hibiscus print tankini that Mom brought me from her pearl trading excursion to Hawaii last year? Too *un*boring.

Graphic tankini that says *KEEP CALM AND SAVE THE OCEANS*? Too…me.

In the end, after trying on nearly every tankini top I own, I settle on one with ruffle straps in a soft kelp green that looks nice with my peachy tailfin *and* just happens to be almost the same shade as Zak's eyes.

Too obvious? Maybe. But for some reason it's having a calming effect. And I need all the calm I can get right now.

I dig through my drawer of hair clips until I find a matching pair. I clamp them in at my temples, hoping they'll at least keep my tangled hair forest mostly out of my face.

By the time I grab my school bag and head downstairs, my room looks like a disaster zone. Some things are unavoidable.

Good thing Mom is out of town and Riatus wouldn't dare venture into my space.

Besides, he's too busy making a gourmet breakfast. I smell the mackerel cakes before I swim into the kitchen. My stomach lets out an angry growl.

"I'm starving," I tell Riatus as I fling my bag toward the front hall.

He looks back over his shoulder. "You're always starving. That's what happens when you have a tapeworm."

"You're hilarious."

I swim up behind him to inspect the breakfast he's putting together.

As far as big brothers go, I don't think I could have done any better. With our mom traveling so much for her work—and our dad gone before I was born—he's had to pick up a lot of the slack at home.

"So where is Mom this week?" I dip my finger into the sweet and spicy sauce that I literally can't wait to pour all over my mackerel cakes. "South Pacific? Indian Ocean? Great Barrier Reef?"

If I didn't know she focuses entirely on work the whole trip, with no time for relaxing or sightseeing, I would be jealous of her travels. Okay, so I'm still jealous.

I'm tired of just reading about other kingdoms. Thalassinia is beautiful, but I want to see more of the ocean. I've begged her to take me, but her answer is always the same: *School first.*

Less than two years to go.

"Eastern Pacific. There's a sea gems convention in Makrianero."

I mentally add that to the list of places I want to go. Which is basically a list of everywhere in the seven seas. And on land. And in outer space.

Just everywhere.

"Do you want sauce on your mackerel cakes?" Riatus doesn't look up from his preparations.

"Do fish poop in the sea?"

That gets his attention.

He glances back over his shoulder and lifts one dark eyebrow. "Is that a yes?"

"Yes, please." I flash him my goofiest grin.

As he goes back to making breakfast, I take a moment to acknowledge my gratitude that he's home. The year he had to be away was one of the hardest in my life.

I know it was awful for Mom, too. Even more than it was for me. But at the time, I thought my life would never come back together.

It has, in all the best ways.

The sand strawberry on top is that Riatus is finally happy. Part of that is being back home, but an even bigger part of it is his relationship with Peri. A relationship that he almost totally blew, by the way, because of some misplaced sense of honor. But thanks to yours truly, they're making it work. I'm so happy for him that I don't even make him say thank you…very often.

I hum quietly to myself while Riatus finishes breakfast.

I've gotten so lost in my own happy thoughts about him that I've completely forgotten the other big thing happening in my life until Riatus sets the platter down in front of me, waits for me to take a giant bite of mackerel cake, and then asks, "So, is there a reason that Zak Marlin is floating outside our front door?"

I nearly choke on my food. Which would be a shame, because it is truly delicious.

Riatus reaches across the table and smacks me hard on the back. "Careful there, champ."

I nod and shake my head at the same time. I can feel

tears stinging my eyes and hope they don't sparkle too much. I take my time chewing and swallowing my food, being extra careful to destroy every teeny, tiny bite.

I'm not avoiding answering his question. Not at all.

When it's all gone, I wash it down with a scoop of lemon-lime jelly.

Maybe, if I take long enough, Riatus will forget about Zak and I can just pretend it—

He cocks a dark eyebrow. "Marlin…?"

No such luck.

"Um, yeah," I dab a napkin to my lips, buying myself a few more precious seconds. "He's, um…here for me."

A second eyebrow joins the first.

Hopefully he thinks my choking incident explains the blush I feel burning at my cheeks. Yeah, totally not because the crush of my life is floating outside, waiting to swim me to school.

I know I made Zak promise not to tell anyone our fake relationship wasn't fake. But if there is one person in this ocean that I can never lie to—who I would never *want* to lie to—it's Riatus.

"We're pretending to date," I blurt.

No response except for those raised eyebrows.

"Angel dumped him," I explain, "but his mom won't stop nagging him about them getting back together." I shrug, as if it's no big deal at all. "So I said we were dating. You know, to, um, help him out."

No one does the stoic silence better than my brother. The Silent Order of Sorranza has nothing on Riatus

37

Ballenato. He just floats there, looking me straight in the eye as if he's peering into my very soul.

"Stop that." I wave my hands in front of my face. "You're freaking me out."

He lowers his eyebrows. "Coral…"

"What?"

He takes a deep breath.

I pretend to be totally engrossed in my platter of mackerel cakes.

"Are you sure this is a good idea?" he asks.

"Why not?" I give him my best totally-confused look. I should win an award.

"Coral, I know you." He leans his forearms on the table and lowers his voice. "I know how you feel about Zak."

My heart pounds against my chest harder than it has since the moment I swam into Zak outside the school on Friday afternoon—which is no small feat, considering how insane my heart goes every time I think about this fake relationship plan.

"I don't know what you mean."

My crush on Zak has been my most carefully guarded secret. Probably my *only* carefully guarded secret.

I'll be honest, I'm not the kind of mergirl anyone should tell secrets. It's not that I have trouble understanding what is secret and what isn't. But often, in the heat of a moment or a conversation, they just seem to…pour out of my mouth.

For four long years I've managed to suppress the overshare when it comes to my crush on Zak.

Those feelings have been in a lockbox, buried deep

beneath the Marianas Trench, the key thrown into the center of the Trigonum Triangle. Too much was riding on that secrecy—my friendship with Zanzia, my relationship with her entire family, my mortal embarrassment.

There is no way I let that slip. No way.

How many other people know this? Does Zanzia? Does *Zak*?! I'll never be able to face anyone ever again.

Riatus must see the rising panic in my eyes because he reaches across the table and lays a hand over mine.

"It was tiny things," he says softly. "The way your eyes light up whenever his name is mentioned, the way you made excuses to go to Zanzia's at every possible opportunity—"

"She's my best friend," I argue.

Riatus smiles gently. "And you're in love with her brother."

My shoulders slump. My entire body slumps.

I'm practically a sea slug in a blob on the floor.

My voice is barely a whisper. "Do you think…?"

I can't finish the question.

Luckily Riatus knows what I want to ask.

"No," he insists. "I'm sure no one else noticed. No one knows."

Well, that's something. A relief. A relief that no one else knows, and also a relief that Riatus does. It's like a tiny bit of the burden of my secret has been lifted.

"About my question," he prods. "Are you sure this fake dating is a good idea?"

"No, of course I'm not sure," I tell him honestly. "But I

couldn't say no. I couldn't just watch him suffer. And I couldn't *not* take the chance that…"

I bite back the words before they can make their way out of my mouth. It's a thought that I haven't even allowed myself to have, let alone speak into the universe. What if I jinx it?

Unfortunately, Riatus doesn't have the same superstition.

"It could turn into something real?" he finishes for me.

There is something so sweet and sympathetic and heart-breaking in how he says it. Now I know my eyes are sparkling with tears that have nothing to do with choking on a sweet and sour mackerel cake.

I take a deep breath to calm my emotions.

I'm surprised when it actually works.

"Maybe it's a mistake," I admit. Because, honestly, we all know that it probably is. "Maybe I'll regret this for the rest of my life." I push my half-empty platter away and float up to my full height. "But if I do, at least I'll know I tried."

A week of fake-dating Zak is a chance I never thought I'd have. I might be a fool to have agreed to this crazy scheme. But I would be an even bigger fool if I let it slip away.

"Just…be careful," Riatus says. "I don't want you to get hurt."

Me neither.

"It already hurts," I tell him. "It has *always* hurt." I give him a half smile. "This can't possibly hurt more."

Riatus doesn't look convinced.

As I grab my bag and head for the front door—for

whatever the world and the waiting merboy outside will bring—I wonder if maybe I'm wrong. Maybe it *can* hurt more.

Only one way to find out.

I pull open the front door and swim out into the day.

FIVE

Monday morning, still

WHEN THE FRONT door closes behind me, it's like I'm leaving my sanity behind. Leaving it safe at home while I swim out into this crazy new world where Zak Marlin —***ZAK MARLIN!***—is waiting to swim me to school.

He's floating casually above the bushes outside the living room window, as if it's a totally normal thing to be doing.

This can't be my real life.

I squeeze my eyes shut and count to ten. This is always how a character in a novel breaks themselves out of a dream, right?

When I re-open my eyes, I fully expect to find Zak gone and me staring up at my bedroom ceiling, wishing the dream would come back.

But nope, there he is, leaning down to inspect the beautiful rose bulb anemones that bloomed overnight, bursting open in a vibrant display of reds, pinks, and purples.

If this is a dream, it's a persistent one.

I've imagined a moment like this countless times, in countless ways. Zak rushing over to see me when he finally realizes that he's been in love with me all this time, too. Zak shyly inviting me to prom because he'd rather go with me than anyone else in the seven seas. Zak coming over unexpectedly for a casual family dinner so we can spend more time together.

All of those crazy fantasy visions of Zak showing up at my house haven't prepared me in any way for the moment when he finally, actually does. Not even a little bit.

His tailfin glistens in the early morning sunlight, the pale purple highlights shimmering against the deep violet scales. He's wearing a dark green UWA Desfleurelle swim shirt that hugs his shoulders just enough to show off his seaball-earned muscles.

And the way he's studying a particularly vibrant anemone bloom makes me smile.

Who wouldn't love a gorgeous, funny, and kind merguy who literally stops to smell the rose bulb anemones?

It would be so easy to let myself sink into this feeling. To forget that I'm only playing along. To pretend, for a little while, that Zak isn't here to get his mom to stop nagging him or to make Angel jealous. To tell myself that the thing I've spent years dreaming about is finally happening.

But that's a dangerous delusion. I can't let myself *actually* believe it, not even for a second.

Because there is one thing the fantasy versions of this

moment I've imagined over the years had that this real one doesn't. In all of them, the feelings Zak had for me were genuine. At least as genuine as the feelings of a fantasy version of someone can be.

In this real version, Zak still only thinks of me as his little sister's best friend. As a friend who's doing him a favor, nothing more.

No matter how much I want it to be genuine, this isn't any more real than my fantasies.

I can't ever forget that.

Pasting on a cheerful, everything-is-totally-fine-and-I'm-not-really-in-love-with-you-at-all smile, I kick away from the door and head for Zak.

"Morning," I call out.

His grin is practically blinding, all bright teeth and crinkled eyes. "Good morning."

My heart wants to melt a little. Okay, my heart wants to melt a *lot*. That is not okay.

I freeze it into an icy, Zak-proof shell. For its own protection.

"Hope you weren't waiting long," I say. "I was running a little behind."

He shrugs, like it doesn't matter to him. "These anemones are beautiful. Do you have a gardener?"

"Uh, no," I say, flustered by the compliment. "Just me."

His eyebrows shoot up.

"Wow, you're super talented." Zak glances back at the bushes one more time before turning his focus on me. "I'm impressed."

"Thanks." I duck my head against the blush that's boiling up my cheeks.

What would Zak do if he knew how much his simple words affect me? Sprint away as fast as he could swim, I'm sure. He'd be back in Desfleurelles before I could blink.

"Are you ready to go?" he asks.

My heart thuds violently against my chest. I don't think I could be *less* ready. Maybe if this was real. But it's not, and I'm still freaking out.

This is my last possible moment to call this whole thing off. I could tell Zak that it was a horrible idea and let's pretend it never happened.

But that small, desperate part of me that wants to spend as much time as physically possible with Zak won't let me fraidy-fish out.

Besides, what kind of friend would I be if I left Zak hanging with no protection against his mom's carping?

So, instead of giving in to the probably-totally-warranted fear racing through my body, I shrug my bag higher onto my shoulder and say, "Ready as I'll ever be."

Zak reaches toward me. Before my poor, Zak-fogged brain can even process what's happening, he lifts my bag off my shoulder.

"I'll carry that." He slings it effortlessly over his shoulder.

I reach for the bag. "You really don't have to."

"It's all part of the show." He winks and then gestures for me to start swimming.

Right. The show.

We're both playing our parts in this charade. Mine

won't be hard—I just have to act like I'm totally head-over-fins for Zak. As if I haven't been practicing that part for years. It will be a much bigger stretch for Zak to play my doting—as he put it—boyfriend. But clearly he's up to the task.

I can't ever forget that everything he does is all part of *the show.*

As we begin the swim to school, my tailfin brushes against Zak's. Instead of moving over or putting space between us, he just winks at me and brushes his tailfin against mine.

"So, um…"

I rack my mind for a safe topic of conversation, desperate for something—*anything*—to distract me from the fact that I am swimming to school with Zak Marlin.

I finally come up with, "How's your speech coming?"

I immediately regret it.

Zak's grin falters and he looks like someone speared him with a harpoon.

"It's *not,*" he says with a groan. "At all. I have no clue where to even start."

"You could always ask Zanzie for help," I suggest. "She's great at speeches."

Zak gives me a wary look. "I asked. She says I shouldn't trust her not to make me sound like an idiot."

I wince. That sounds about right. Zanzie wouldn't do it maliciously—she's not that kind of person—but she does have a mischievous streak. She might think it'd be a hilarious prank.

"Can we just not talk about it?" he asks.

He sounds almost as miserable as he did last night when his mom was nagging him about Angel.

"Sure," I say. "Of course."

We swim on in silence.

I feel bad for even bringing up the speech. I know how much he hates public speaking. I should have known.

The silence is starting to feel awkward—or maybe it's just me—but I don't want to risk saying something else upsetting. My mental faculties aren't exactly churning at full speed right now.

Thankfully, Zak is much better at finding safe topics of conversation. "So how's your family?"

"Good," I say with a huge sigh of relief. "They're good."

"Good."

He smiles and keeps on swimming. But I'm not about to fall back into that uncomfortable silence. Latching onto the conversation lifeline, I keep the topic going.

"My mom is in Makrianero for a pearl convention," I tell him.

"Makrianero?" He looks at me, clearly intrigued. "That's in the Northeast Pacific, right?"

"Have you ever been?"

He shakes his head.

"Me neither."

But Mom has described it to me in detail. I picture the green, vibrant world she's described to me. All kelp forests and coldwater sea life. As different from Thalassinia as a shark is from a seahorse

"I've heard it's breathtakingly lush up there," I sigh.

"It's supposed to be one of the most popular tourist destinations in the seven seas."

"Mom has told me so many stories about the different kingdoms around the world." I do a little joyful twirl in the water. "When I graduate, I'm going to spend a year traveling the oceans with her before I go to college."

"That sounds amazing." Zak stares dreamily ahead. "I've always wanted to see the world."

I gasp. "Me too! All of it!"

"If I could," he says, "I would pack a sack with the barest necessities and spend a year swimming wherever the current takes me."

I can almost taste the freedom. "No homework, no responsibilities."

"No speeches in front of the entire school." He huffs out a little laugh at himself.

My imagination races. "Finding pirate treasure."

"Seeing sights that no merperson has ever seen."

"That sounds…"

"That would be…"

"Perfect," we both say.

Then we both sigh, each lost in envisioning our own version of the traveling nomad fantasy.

Okay, that's probably what Zak's doing. Dreaming of current-surfing around the world, from one pole to the other.

I, on the other hand, am wondering how on earth I didn't know this about him. Four long years of noting every teeny-tiny detail I could learn about him, and I had no idea that he wants to travel as much as I do.

Guess I'm not as good at this crush thing as I thought.

"Why don't you?" I suggest.

Zak looks at me, startled. "Why don't I what?"

"Travel the world?" I flash him a smile. "You're legally an adult. You could just…go."

Even as I say it, I wish I hadn't. Because if Zak goes traveling around the globe, I'll see him even less than I do now.

Luckily, he's not about to pack up and swim away.

He snorts out a dismissive laugh. "Have you met my parents?"

"Yeah, true. They're a bit…"

"Great, definitely. But also…. They have certain ideas about what I should be doing with my life." He shrugs. "I pick my battles."

I smile. "Like the break-up?"

"Exactly."

In all of my years crushing on Zak from afar, my fantasies about him have swum the spectrum. Some of them were big scale fantasies. Like him knocking on my window in the middle of the night to say he'd sunk more and more in love with me every day and couldn't wait one second longer to tell me.

But most of them, the vast majority, were little daydreams. Imagining little moments of connection. Like this one.

Swimming side-by-side, talking about things that matter. Talking about our plans and dreams. Floating along in silence—awkward or not. Just…being together.

This is what dating Zak would have been like.

I shake that thought out of my head as quickly as it appears. There's no use crying over a wave that's already crashed against the shore. If he was ever going to feel anything romantic for me, he would by now. Zak and I are obviously destined to be nothing more than friends. And I can be okay with that.

Mostly.

Still, a mergirl could get used to this.

Until we swim around a corner and Queen Sirenia Academy comes into view. The blue and green sea fans that decorate the roof fluttering in the early morning current. Reality crashes into me like a blue whale on a mission.

My heart rate triples.

I've made this swim countless times. There have been plenty of days over the years that I've wanted to turn around and swim home. I still remember the fear of the unknown as I swam in for my first day of school. Other times I had a big test I didn't feel ready for or a homework assignment I forgot or a big presentation to freak out over. The first time I had to face Zak after I realized how I felt about him had been super nerve-wracking.

But I've never been more terrified than I am right now.

Telling the Marlins last night and Riatus this morning was one thing. Telling the entire school is a whole different thing.

"I can't do this." I pull to an abrupt stop.

Zak stops next to me, a small line creasing between his brows. "Why not?"

"I'm a terrible liar. I'll never be able to pull it off."

He swims closer, so close that I can smell the aftershave cream he uses. It smells like sargassum and coconut.

"Of course you can," he says with a laugh. "All you have to do is follow my lead."

"It's not too late," I insist. "No one outside of family knows. You can just swim home, and we'll pretend like this never happened."

I place my hands on his chest and try to push him away. Which has the obvious consequence of my hands being on his chest. I pull my hands back as if they've been burned.

I'm too freaked out to enjoy the contact.

He swims closer still, so close I can feel the heat of his body swirling around me like a fuzzy blanket.

I inhale deeply, drawing his scent into me. It calms me. *He* calms me.

"You can do this," he says softly. "The key is to focus on the truth within the lie."

I feel myself relaxing, lulled by the gentle tone of his voice. My anxiety starts ebbing away.

"Think of it this way," he says, his voice barely more than a whisper. "Most of it is true. We have a relationship."

"We're just friends," I remind him. And myself.

Mostly myself.

"That's still a relationship." He smiles. "And we are really going to Give Back Week events together."

I give him a weak smile. "That's true."

"So the only part that's a lie," he says, "is that we're madly in love with each other."

The laugh bubbles out of me before I can stop it. Zak has no idea how close to home that hits.

While that statement might be the lie for him. For me, that's the closest thing to true in this entire situation. I'm not sure whether that's somewhat reassuring or totally alarming.

He floats there, barely a few inches away, his smile and his gaze steady.

He's so confident, so convincing.

That's Zak. Steady, confident, convincing. He believes he can't fail.

Of course it will work out for him. Everything always does. He's Zak freaking Marlin. QSA's golden boy—literally. There is a golden statue of him in the trophy case.

He is the most perfect student to ever swim QSA's halls.

And that's the problem. I didn't realize it until this exact instant, but that's the real reason I want to call this whole thing off.

I close my eyes and force myself to voice my deepest fear.

"*Who will believe it?*"

I whisper the question so softly I doubt he even heard me. When he stays silent, I'm sure that he didn't.

Opening my eyes, I look him straight in his kelp-green eyes.

"Who will ever believe that *Zak Marlin* is in love with *Coral Ballenato?*"

No one.

He shakes his head and smiles so big that I can't help but smile in return. *That* smile is his superpower.

He takes both of my hands in his.

"Who will believe it?" he echoes. "*Everyone.*"

Shivers race down my spine. I'm not sure if it's because he's holding my hands or because he said that with so much sincerity that even *I* want to believe.

Before I can decide which, he releases one of my hands and keeps the other clasped tightly in his as he starts swimming for school. He's not letting me turn back. As the heat of his palm against mine warms me from the inside out, I don't want to do anything except follow wherever he swims.

Ready or not, this is happening.

SIX

Monday afternoon

TALK ABOUT ANTI-CLIMACTIC. No one even noticed me
swimming up to school with Zak. He seemed disappointed,
but I was thrilled. Anything to put off the impossible task of
having to convince someone—anyone—that this is real.

So my morning pretty much went along as usual.

By lunchtime, I've practically forgotten about the
arrangement with Zak altogether. If by forgotten I mean
I've reviewed and overanalyzed every single moment of our
swim to school together in excruciating, exhausting detail.

So, yeah, *not* forgotten.

I am, however, hoping that Zanzia has managed to
forget. It's possible, right? She's slept since then and we don't
have any morning classes together, so lunch is the first time
I'll see her since dinner last night.

Maybe she'll have had some other major life drama that makes her forget everything else that's going on.

And maybe I'll set up a pearl shop on the moon.

This is going to be bad. I have to grip my lunch tray harder to keep my hands from shaking. I'm not prepared for this.

I get to our table first, as always.

We selected *our table* very carefully on the first day of Year Nine. Zanzia likes to be in the center—of everything: attention, the universe, the room. I prefer to stick to the edges, not quite out of the mix, but nowhere near in the middle of it. So we compromised with the table closest to the doors.

Zanzie likes it because literally *everyone* has to pass by our table to get into the cafeteria.

I like it because I can make a quick escape if I have to. And not just in case of a humiliating high school experience. Imagining and planning my response in the case of a merzombie apocalypse may or may not be one of my hobbies.

I've just settled my tray on the table when I feel the water chill around me as Zanzia floats down across from me and slams her tray onto the stone surface. Clearly she hasn't forgotten about me and Zak either.

"Tell me everything," she says without preamble.

I hastily shove a bite of seaweed salad into my mouth. Since it would be rude to speak with food in my mouth, I mime: *What?*

"Puh-lease." She stabs a juicy kelpberry with a seastick.

"Don't play dumb with me. We both know you know exactly what I'm talking about."

I swallow hard. The seaweed salad is clearly not a strong enough barrier against Zanzia on a mission. The Great Wall of Kentrikatos couldn't stop Zanzia.

This will be the hardest part.

Zanzie and I have been best friends for years, and I try to never, ever lie to her. I try to never, ever lie to anyone, but not only is Zanzie like a sister to me, she is also a genuine merfolk lie detector. Nothing gets past her.

The only time I've knowingly and convincingly lied to her was about where my brother went for the year he was gone. I had to lie to everyone about that.

Which actually cheers me up a little. I did this once before. I can do it again.

The fact that the lie is about me and Zak shouldn't make a difference. Right? My stomach flip-flops.

Great, I can't even lie to myself.

I can do this. I just need to play it confident.

I channel my inner Zanzia and give her a casual shrug.

"I don't know, it just kind of…happened."

Which is actually true. Like Zak said, keep the story as close to the truth as possible.

Her eyes narrow. "Explain."

She shoves the kelpberry in her mouth, watching me closely as I scramble for an answer.

"Well, um…" I try hard to remember the story I rehearsed in my brain last night—over and over and over. It seemed so easy when I said it in my head. "We ran into each other outside school on Friday. We started talking."

She lifts her brows in a *duh* expression.

I throw her my best *I'm-getting-to-it* look in response.

"We started talking about the Give Back Week events. You know, the game and the carnival and the—"

"I know about the Give Back Week events," Zanzie says with an eye roll. "Get to the part where you are suddenly dating my brother."

My heart starts racing. Time for the whopper.

"Zak asked if I was going to the events with anyone, and when I said I wasn't, he asked if I wanted to go with him." I shrug as nonchalantly as possible. "I said *yes*."

That's the story Zak and I agreed on and I'm sticking to it. Who cares if I spit the words out so fast they were practically glued together?

I force a bite of food into my mouth while Zanzia studies me. If my mouth is full, that buys me time to answer the next question.

Her piercing violet eyes bore laser holes into my brain. The longer she stares at me, the more I freak out inside. If mermaids could sweat, I'd be doing it in buckets.

Panicked thoughts race through my mind. *Can she tell that I'm lying? She seems unconvinced. Maybe I said something to give it all away. Maybe I need to explain more. Maybe explaining more will make it seem even less convincing. What am I going to do???*

In the end, she lifts a plump hamachi roll with her seasticks and says, "You're a terrible liar," before popping it into her mouth.

I try to sound confused, which is really hard to do when your heart is pounding into your throat.

"I don't know what you—"

"Zak already told me the truth," she says.

My jaw drops. "What? He promised me he wouldn't tell anyone we're faking, not even—"

"Ha, I knew it!" Zanzia leans triumphantly onto the table. "I knew you were lying."

It takes me seven full heartbeats to realize what she's saying. Scuttlebutt. I am such a dorkfish. My shoulders slump.

"Zak didn't tell you anything," I sigh, "did he?"

Zanzia grins as she shakes her head. "Not a word."

Of course I fell for it. I'm not surprised. Like I said, Zanzia is the sea queen of deception. I'm only surprised that she tricked me into revealing the truth so quickly. I didn't even last one lunch period.

I thought I would at least make it through the school day.

I rush around to her side of the table.

"Promise me you won't tell anyone, Z," I whisper fervently.

She looks offended that I even have to say it. But I have too much at stake to just trust her innate sense of secrecy.

"I don't want to be the school joke," I explain.

Her indignant expression turns completely serious. Zanzia may love to be overly dramatic, but she knows how to turn it off when something is really important.

"No one will hear it from me." She traces a cross over her heart. "Promise."

Smiling, I release a huge sigh of relief.

Well that's one less thing to worry about. Plus, there's

the added bonus of not having to keep this secret from Zanzie. It will be so much easier with her on my side.

"Tell me about this plan," she says, back to swirling her lunch around with her seasticks. "What are you guys even thinking?"

I give her the quick rundown—leaving out the part about my years-long crush on her brother and keeping my voice as low as possible to prevent anyone around us from overhearing.

When I've finished explaining, she stares at me, unblinking, for several seconds before saying, "So, basically, you've entered into a marriage of convenience."

"What?! No, we're not getting married."

Not that an image of me swimming down the aisle in a white gown with Zak waiting at the other end in a lavender tuxedo jacket doesn't immediately pop into my mind.

Zanzia bursts out laughing. "Of course not. But you're entering into a fake relationship that benefits both of you."

"Yeah, I guess…"

"Standard marriage of convenience plot. It's one of my favorite romance tropes." She cocks her head to one side, sending her magenta hair swirling that direction. "I know what Zak is getting out of this. Poseidon knows I've done way crazier things to get Mom off my back."

I laugh awkwardly. Inside, I kind of cringe. Mrs. Marlin can be kind of over the top, but at least she's home all the time.

Don't get me wrong. I love my mom more than anything. I just wish she didn't have to spend so many nights out on the current.

"What I don't know," Zanzie continues, "is what *you* get."

That explosion just heard around the world? It's my heart rate jumping into hyper-speed. If I get out of this whole fake-dating thing without having a heart attack, it will be a miracle.

"Isn't it obvious?" I ask, deflecting.

Zanzia narrows her eyes again, studying me for any clue or sign or telepathic message—honestly, who can tell with her.

Apparently not discerning or divining anything, she says, "Spell it out."

"A date?" Great. Why did that sound like a question? I push a piece of ahi around on my plate. "For Give Back Week."

She barks out the loudest, sharpest laugh ever.

I glance around to see if she's drawn anyone else's attention. Luckily, the student body of QSA seems occupied with its own dramas.

"First of all—" Zanzie holds up one finger, ticking things off on her verbal list. "—you could care less about having a date for Give Back Week. We always go to everything together. Second—" Another finger. "—you could go with pretty much any merguy in school if you wanted to."

I'm not sure whether to be embarrassed or stunned by that proclamation.

"And third," she continues, "we both know it's because you've been head-over-fins in L-O-V-E with my brother since Year Seven."

My jaw couldn't possibly drop any lower.

She waggles her three fingers at me.

I grab her hand and pull myself close to her. "How did you— Why didn't you— How long—"

"Chill, drama queen." Her face softens into a sympathetic expression. "You're not exactly going to win actress of the year. I've *always* known."

My mind races through every single interaction I've had with Zanzia and Zak over the years, desperately searching for the moment that gave me away. I tried so hard—*so hard!*—from the very beginning to keep it secret.

Not that it matters now. She knows, and all I care about is that she doesn't think I'm friends with her for any reason other than *her*.

"You're my best best friend. That has nothing to do with—"

"I know." She flashes me that brilliant Marlin grin. "That's one of the reasons I love you so much."

With that one sentence, she reassures me that everything will be okay between us. I sigh out a huge rush of relief.

In all these years of loving Zak from afar, the thought of Zanzia finding out was one of my biggest fears. Second biggest, actually. Right after Zak finding out. When every single giddy guppy part of me wanted nothing more than to gush about my crush to my best friend, I fought to keep that secret locked in tight. Because Zanzia's friendship means more to me than anything, and I would never want to do anything to jeopardize that.

Realizing that she's known all along and is still my best friend means more to me than I can possibly say.

"I'm sorry," I tell her. "I wish...." I shake my head, but no brilliant thoughts click into place. "I wish I didn't."

"Why? You should never be sorry for love." She picks up another kelpberry. "I just don't want you to get hurt. I'm not sure I'm equipped to deal with a heartbroken Coral."

Me neither.

"It's only for a week," I tell her. "I'll be fine."

Zanzia opens her mouth to say something more—probably not something I want to hear at this point—but before she can speak, someone appears at our table.

I look up and find Chromis Monkfish hovering over me.

"Hi, Chromis." I flash him a smile. "What's up?"

Chromis and I aren't exactly friends, but we're in a lot of the same classes and he's president of the school's Environmental Club. Most of our interactions have been about homework or club activities.

He pushes his glasses up the bridge of his nose.

"Please forgive the interruption," he says, glancing nervously at Zanzia and then back at me. "But I wished to speak with you concerning a personal matter. May I?"

I flash Zanzie a confused look. She only shrugs.

"Sure," I say. "What is it?"

"As I'm sure you are aware, the school's Give Back Week festivities will take place this coming week."

I smile gently. "Yes, I'm aware."

"The activities present several opportunities for social interaction."

Out of the corner of my eye, I see Zanzia clap a hand over her mouth.

I ignore her. "Yes…"

"Would you do me the honor of attending one or more of these festivities with me?" He clears his throat. "As my date?"

My jaw drops.

Did that just happen? Did Chromis Monkfish just ask me out?

Judging by the nervous, half-strangled look on his face, I think the answer is *yes*. Yes he did.

Despite Zanzie's dubious declaration that I could go out with any merguy in school if I wanted, the sad truth is that my not wanting isn't the only reason I haven't dated. No one has ever asked me.

Which, I know, wouldn't stop me from being the one to ask. But considering my aforementioned-multiple-times, all-encompassing crush, I never have.

This is a first.

"Oh, Chromis, that's so sweet." I genuinely mean it. If the whole thing with Zak hadn't happened, I would probably say yes. "But I'm already going with someone."

He blinks several times before asking, "Who?"

My heart lurches into my throat. This is it. The first time I'm actually going to say it out loud. To someone who isn't family or like family.

No turning back.

I draw in a deep, fortifying breath. Flash a quick glance at Zanzie, who gives me an encouraging nod.

"Zak Marlin."

My voice is soft, tentative, as if I'm afraid to speak the

words into existence. But I know that I can't show doubt if I want people to believe this.

So I gather as much confidence as I can and say, "I'm going with Zak Marlin."

The words come out way louder than I expected.

Chromis blinks so much I think there might be something wrong with his eyes. I'm just about to suggest that he go see the nurse when he finally nods.

"Oh." Blink-blink. "Perhaps another time."

Then, before I can say, *Yes, I'd like that*, he spins and swims away.

I watch him go, a half-smile of confusion on my face. That was weird. Sweet, but weird.

Then Zanzie clears her throat loudly enough to draw my attention back to our table. Her eyes are wide and her eyebrows are doing some kind of wild, don't-look-around dance.

But I do. I do look around.

That's when I realize that the entire lunchroom has fallen silent. The students at the tables nearest us are staring at me in various expressions of shock, awe, and confusion. I watch as they turn to each other and start whispering.

The next ring of tables repeats the cycle. And then the next.

I've never been a topic for the gossip mill. I glance at Zanzia. She has way more experience being in the eye of the hurricane.

This is bad.

I spin back around to face her. "How long until Angel hears?"

"At the rate this news is spreading?" Zanzia glances around the lunchroom. "I'd say in about five... four...three..."

I glance back over my shoulder. Watching, as the wave of gossip spreads through the student body like squid ink in a whirlpool.

From table to table to table to table.

All the way from our spot by the door to the biggest table in the far corner. The popular table. Angel's table.

I can see the moment the news reaches her.

Angel's head snaps up and she scans the room until she spots me. She stares straight at me. Into me. *Through* me.

Then, as my heart threatens to race right out of my chest, Angel floats up from her table and swims straight for me, her long blond hair flowing behind her like a cape. I've never been in a fight at school. Or a fight anywhere. I hide from conflict like a flounder camouflaging itself against the sand so the sharks swim right on by.

I sense Zanzia stiffen. She, on the other hand, loves a good fight—verbal *or* physical. She'll have my back.

I brace myself for the confrontation.

Instead of stopping at our table to confront me, though, Angel swims right past us and out the lunchroom door, leaving a sea of confused and disappointed students in her wake.

I can't overstate how relieved I am. I know that helping Zak make Angel jealous is part of the whole plan, but I didn't really think ahead to what she might do when she found out.

All things considered, I got off easy.

"That could have gone worse," I say with a relieved smile.

The expression Zanzie gives me tells me nothing I don't already know. I may have avoided the clash with Angel for now, but she won't let it go forever. I'll have to face her before Give Back Week is over.

I'll just have to be prepared when she comes for me.

SEVEN

Tuesday night

FOR MOST OF my years in school, I've managed to swim under the radar of the rumor mill and gossip circle. Except for that one time in Year Eight when *someone—cough-Zanzia-cough*—started a rumor that I had bonded to Prince Allrik of Glacialis.

I freaked out so much from the intense attention that I had to stay home from school for a week.

Amazingly, I have now survived an entire two days as the center of everything anyone at school is talking about without having a debilitating anxiety attack. Clearly, I have matured.

At some point between that moment in the cafeteria and now, I think every single merperson in school—including several teachers—has asked me about Zak. Some just want to know how Zak is doing, if he likes college, and whether he's going to be at the game. This is what happens when the most popular merguy in school is also one of the nicest.

Others are clearly curious about how awkward, driven, science nerd Coral Ballenato snagged the most perfect merguy in school history. Since I can't exactly say, *I didn't, we're just faking it to get his mom off his back about his ex-girlfriend*, I just giggle and shrug and say, *I know, right?!*

Everyone has asked me about Zak. Everyone, that is, except Angel and her inner circle. From them I've gotten blank stares and dirty looks.

Which I totally don't understand because *she* broke up with *him*. How am I the bad mergirl here?

Honestly, I don't know how she handled the constant attention and turmoil of being his girlfriend. Not only is it exhausting, but with every moment Zak and I spend together, I feel the too-long-crushing-from-afar part of me doing a celebration dance.

There have been a *lot* of those moments. Zak has swum me to and from school each day. And, if I'm being honest, swimming with him is the best part of my day.

We always manage to find something to talk about, whether it's how much harder college classes are, the deteriorating environmental state of the oceans, or even just throwing around ideas for what we're going to do at the carnival. I feel like I could talk to him forever and never get bored.

That is both wonderful and terrifying.

Wonderful for obvious reasons, I suppose.

Terrifying because I want this all-too-temporary feeling

—this all-too-temporary romantic relationship—to last forever.

Which is why, when Zak met me after school earlier and suggested we go out for dinner at a super-popular sushi place, I said I would have to meet him there. I did actually have a project to work on, but that wasn't the only reason I didn't swim away with him then and there.

Spending time together in places where people will see us is obviously important for *the show*. But it's hard on my heart. Keeping my crush in check has to be priority number one.

To do that, sometimes I'll have to put some time and space between us.

This is what I keep repeating to myself as I sit at the table, waiting for Zak to arrive. I've had these conversations with myself a lot over the years. Get over him. Let it go. Move on. Fall in love with someone else.

It's never worked.

It's never been more important that I succeed.

Something shifts in the water around me. In an instant, there is a ripple of energy that washes across the entire restaurant.

I know before I look up that Zak has arrived. He has that effect on people. Rooms light up, people smile, oceans part, and sea nymphs dance on golden waves.

Okay, maybe I'm being a little overdramatic. But his presence has a palpable effect on whatever space he occupies.

I look up and see him floating just inside the entrance, smiling at the host. He claps the young merman on the shoulder, thanks him, and then swims straight for me.

My heart rate triples.

Dear self, this is not how you keep a crush in check.

By the time he reaches our table, I've calmed my breathing and cooled the water around me to counteract the blush I just know is creeping up my cheeks.

I can't keep the goofy smile off my face, though. The Zak Effect is too strong.

"Sorry I'm late."

He swims close and presses a quick kiss to my cheek. I'm amazed the water around me doesn't boil on contact.

"You're not," I manage to say as he floats down to his seat. "I was early."

"I try to be early. It never works out."

I can imagine. Zak can't swim five feet without someone stopping him to talk. It's astonishing he got from the entrance to our table without a lengthy conversation about the school's chances in the kingdom seaball tournament this year.

"Sometimes I try to be late," I tell him. "It never works out either."

He laughs, and I feel it all the way to the tip of my tailfin.

Warning! Dangerous waters ahead.

"So tell me about this big project," he says. "Is it top secret?"

I shrug. "Not really. The environmental club is decorating recycle bins to place around school."

"Cool. That's going to make a big difference."

"Hi there!" A cheerful server swims up to our table. "How are you two love birds doing?"

My throat cinches shut.

Zak doesn't have the same reaction. "We're great. How are you?"

The server, a mergirl not more than a few years older than us, blushes. At least I'm not the only one who has that reaction around Zak.

"I'm terrific, thanks for asking." She nods at the menus on our table. "Do you know what you want?"

"I always know what I want," Zak replies.

He looks at me, his eyes sparkling, and for a split-second it feels like he's talking about me. I have to be imagining that, right?

I open my mouth to say…something. Anything. Nothing comes out.

"How about the King Whelk Platter?" he suggests.

I nod. At least, I *think* I nod. I attempt the movement, but I'm not sure it actually happens.

"Great," Zak says. He looks up at the server. "The King Whelk Platter."

She scribbles something on her pad and then swims off to place our order.

"Carp," Zak says. "I forgot the King Whelk has *hamaguri* rolls. I hate *hamaguri*."

"*Hamaguri*?" I echo, relieved to find my voice is still working. "I love *hamaguri*."

Zak smiles so big I feel my crush on him burning through the ice cage I've locked it away in.

"Clearly we're a perfect pair," he says.

I cough to cover my attempt to shove my crush back down where it belongs before it crashes out into the water around me. This is going to be harder than I thought.

"So, um…" I grasp for something to change the subject. "Tell me about your day. What did you do?"

I instantly regret the question. His brows drop low over his eyes and all trace of that smile disappears.

"I was working on my speech," he says.

I wince. "That bad?"

He groans. "Why couldn't Coach have just asked me to play in the game instead?" He scrubs his hands over his face. "Or hand out energy bars. Or even do the stadium cleanup after the game. Anything would be better than having to give a speech."

My stomach knots up for him. I've never felt this kind of stress about public speaking. For some reason, I don't have any trouble presenting to huge groups of people. I just tend to freak out a little if they all try to come talk to me at once afterward. It's the individual attention I can't handle.

But for Zak this is like the seventh circle of Hades.

"You'll give a great speech," I cheer. Because he will. He's great at everything he does. "You just need to practice until you feel comfortable."

"I know you're right." He flashes me a grateful smile. "But right now it feels like I could practice for years and still not be ready."

My hand instinctively starts to reach out to take his, to reassure him that he'll get through this challenge. But I stop. Mentally chastising myself for almost blowing it. This isn't real. I can't let myself act like it is.

Then the most magical thing happens.

Zak moves his hand toward mine.

Before I know what's happening, he has turned my hand over and pressed our palms together.

The contact sends an electric flash straight to my heart. I might not survive this night. I definitely won't survive this week.

There is a goofy smile on my face, I just know it.

"Aren't you two, cute?" Our server swirls up to the table, a large plate perched on one hand. "One King Whelk Platter. I asked them to throw on a couple of extra *oshinko maki.*"

She winks at Zak, who smiles back with genuine gratitude.

"You're the best," he replies.

She giggles a little and then swims away.

I get it, girl. Zak has that effect on everyone. Male, female. Young, old. Everything in between. He is the definition of charming.

I have to minimize the effect on me.

Zak picks up his seasticks in one hand, not releasing his hold on mine with the other.

"I...sorry." I awkwardly pull my hand away. "I can't operate my seasticks left-handed."

He just smiles and shakes his head as he pops an *oshinko maki* into his mouth.

I pick up a *hamaguri* roll and look away as I direct it into my mouth. I'm not sure I could actually eat while looking Zak in the eyes. One of two things would happen: either I would laugh so hard I couldn't get the food into my mouth in the first place, or the roll would get stuck in my throat and I would die before I get to fully enjoy this night with him.

But the downside of looking away from him is that my gaze lands on the front door.

More specifically on the blonde mergirl floating up to the hostess stand.

It's a miracle I don't choke on my *hamaguri*.

"What's wrong?" Zak asks, apparently sensing my distress.

I swallow hard. "Nothing, it's just…" I give him a wary look. "Angel is here."

He twists around to look at her. His entire body tenses. He must see what I see: that Angel isn't alone. She's here with Tomtate Sargeant.

When Zak turns back to face me, he looks a little pale. No wonder. Not only did Angel dump him, but she's already moved on. I can't imagine how it feels to see your ex with a new merguy.

But I *can* imagine how to feels to see someone you care about with someone else. I've spent the last four years feeling that way. I can totally empathize.

"We can go," I offer. "Maybe try somewhere else?"

He shakes his head. "No. It's fine."

He flashes me a smile as he reaches across the table, taking my left hand in his. I can tell it's not a full-on smile.

This whole arrangement isn't about me, though. It's about helping Zak out. It's about making Angel jealous, and we can't exactly do that if we flee whenever we see her.

My heart, though? My heart is determined to believe

that this is real. It pounds in my chest as if excited that I'm finally getting what I've spent so long dreaming of.

And I can't even be mad at it.

I know this is going to end badly. Zak is still in love with his ex-girlfriend. We're only fake dating for a few more days, and then he'll be back in college and I'll be left to pick up the pieces of my crush-broken heart.

But that's a price I'm willing to pay to feel like this in the meantime.

Which means there is only one thing to do. Enjoy every single moment while I can.

I squeeze Zak's hand a little tighter and pop another bite into my mouth.

I'll worry about the consequences later.

EIGHT

Wednesday afternoon

THE GIVE BACK Week carnival is possibly the best thing that happens in Thalassinia all year. The school transforms the empty plot of sand next to the seaball field into an amusement park. There are rides and games and every possible type of food stall you can imagine.

My favorite has always been the karaoke stage. Merfolk who don't know me that well usually find it surprising. I don't know how to explain it. While I might not usually be as wild and daring as my best friend, for some reason singing along with my favorite songs makes me feel alive.

When Zanzia and I won Best Duo two years ago, I thought life couldn't get any better.

I was wrong.

Going to the carnival with Zak is infinitely better.

Plus, it's going to be stress-free because I overheard

Angel telling her friends that she thought the carnival was only for guppies and losers. Which, assuming she doesn't consider herself either of those things, means she won't be here.

Maybe I should have mentioned that to Zak—what's the point of us going together if she's not going to see us and get jealous—but…I'm being selfish about it. I want to enjoy my time with Zak to the max.

And boy have we been enjoying ourselves.

First thing, we rode the Torpedo Whirl. Which, if you've never been to an underwater carnival, let me describe for you. It's a dolphin-shaped pod just big enough for two, attached by a long arm to a column in the center. Zak and I swim into the pod on our stomachs and hold onto a bar in the front. Once we're belted in for safety, the operator hits a button and we shoot through the water like a torpedo from a submarine.

The ride doesn't last long enough, only about five times around the track, but it is literally The. Most. Fun.

After the Torpedo Whirl, we moved on to the arcade.

Zak played bubble darts so well that he won me a giant stuffed starfish.

I played balloon harpoon so, um, *not* well that I won him a tiny stuffed sea cucumber.

Since then, we've ridden the Torpedo Whirl again, stuffed ourselves with calamari cakes and shrimp-on-a-stick, entered the three-armed-swim race, and now we're back in line for another trip on the Torpedo Whirl.

I can't remember ever having more fun. Not in my entire life. Zak makes me laugh like a goldfish with the giggles. He's kind and generous and makes everyone around him feel a little bit better.

That ice cage that I'd constructed around my crush? Around my poor, vulnerable heart? Yeah, shattered into oblivion.

I never want this feeling to end.

It's going to. I know it's going to. We're almost at the end of the third day, with just three more days to go. Halfway over already.

The clock is ticking.

Every time that thought bubbles to the surface of my mind, I shove it way back down. I refuse to waste one single moment of what little time we have left. Never let it be said that Coral Ballenato didn't *carpe diem*.

"Next up," the Torpedo Whirl operator shouts.

Zak flashes me a wickedly excited grin. "Ladies first."

I spin around in a circle of fake astonishment. "No ladies around here. Just me."

"Then I guess you'll—"

"Race ya!" I shout before he can finish.

I kick off with all my power, leaving Zak in a storm of bubbles. I'm halfway to the pod when he catches me. I feel his hand on my tailfin, wrapping around the narrow stem to restrict my kicking.

"Hey, no fair," I cry.

He pulls up even with me and winks. "Who ever said I was fair?"

I pretend to be outraged.

But Zak is fair. He's one of the fairest merpeople I've ever met. I've seen it countless times—on the seaball field, in the halls at school, interacting with random merfolk in public.

That's just one of the reasons that everyone loves him.

It's just one of the reasons that *I* love him.

My face falls a little bit at the bittersweet thought.

"Hey, if it makes you feel better," he says, his tone slightly heavier, "next time I'll let you win."

For a competitive athlete like Zak, that's a major concession. Rather than give in to the sentimental smile that I feel tugging at my lips, I twist my mouth into a smirk.

"Next time, I'll beat you fair and square."

While he throws his head back in a huge laugh, I take advantage of his distraction to race the rest of the way to the pod.

"Never mind," I call out to him, "I'll just beat you this time."

Zak joins me in the pod, still laughing.

"And here I always thought you were a *good mergirl*," he says with a smile. "I never knew you had such a devious streak."

"There's a lot you don't know about me," I say as I buckle myself into the pod.

I meant that to come out joking, but it ended up sounding kind of wistful. When I look up, Zak is staring at me with the most intense gaze, his kelp green eyes burning into me.

His voice is low and serious as he says, "I know there is."

My breath catches.

"Are you two lovebirds ready?" the ride operator calls out.

His intrusion breaks the weird tension filling the pod. Suddenly needing something to do with my hands, I quickly reach around Zak to pull his belt around his waist. Then I wrap my fingers around the bar at the front of the pod. Zak does the same, except he covers my left hand with his right.

"Coral, I—"

Before he can finish that sentence, our pod shoots off, sending us speeding through the water. This is what I imagine flying feels like. Or maybe skydiving.

It's exhilarating.

By the time the ride finishes, Zak's hand is off mine so he can hold onto the bar for dear life. Honestly, my heart is pounding hard enough already. It couldn't take the extra stress of Zak holding my hand anyway.

"I think he sent us around extra times," I say breathlessly as we start the swim back to the entrance.

Zak grins as he presses a hand to his head. "I'm so dizzy I can't swim straight."

We both try to move in a straight line but end up weaving back and forth like a pair of terrapeds who are just learning how to swim. Zak tries to reach for my arm, but his aim is off so bad that he misses me and sends himself into a spin.

I start laughing and can't stop. To see Mr. Seaball Superstar, the perfect athlete, struggling to even swim in a straight line is, for some reason, the funniest thing I've ever seen.

Soon Zak is laughing too. We're practically doing barrel rolls as we make our way back to the main swimway of the carnival.

"Hey, if it isn't the very couple we were looking for!"

I twist around at the sound of Zanzia's voice and barely keep my jaw from dropping.

I'm not sure what shocks me more: the fact that Zanzia just called me and Zak a couple, or that her magenta hair is now striped with streaks of blue and purple. When did that happen?

Since she's in on the secret about our fake relationship, I'm definitely going to give the edge to her ever-evolving hair color.

Zanzia swims toward us, her variety show co-chair, Goby Grunion, following in her wake.

"Zanzia!" Zak puts his arm around my shoulder as we all meet in front of the shell toss booth. "My favorite sister."

"Your only sister," she says.

He grins and squeezes me closer. "Exactly."

I can't decide if I should give in to the urge to put my arm around Zak's waist. It feels like the most natural thing in the world to do, but also like the most awkward at the same time.

In the end I just clasp my hands together in front of me.

"You were looking for us?" I ask.

"Yes!" Zanzie wiggles with excitement. "They've doubled the karaoke stage this year. We want to do a group sing."

"Sounds great." I try to pull away from Zak, but he's holding on tight. "Zak?"

He swallows nervously.

Zanzia crosses her arms over her chest. She doesn't say anything, but it's clearly a challenge.

"Sure," he says, although he sounds anything but. "Let's do it."

Zak holds my hand as we follow Zanzia and Goby to the stage. There is a group just finishing up as Zanzia swims over to the host to give them our names.

While we wait for them to cue up our song—an upbeat number from Makrianero boy band Mer Magic Max—Zak looks nervous. I can only imagine that his fear of public speaking includes singing.

"You don't have to do this," I whisper.

"I never back down from a challenge," he whispers back. "But I should probably warn you that I'm a terrible singer."

I shake my head. No way. I don't believe Zak Marlin is terrible at anything.

Then, before I can argue, the music begins.

Zanzia takes the first lead, singing at the top of her lungs. She's been in choir since forever and musical theatre for the last three years. Her voice is amazing. Which is good, because everyone in the kingdom can probably hear her.

Then Goby takes his turn. He's been doing musical theatre for longer than Zanzia, so his singing is even better.

Then he passes the megaphone to me.

It's one of my favorite songs. Whenever I hear it, it's like they're singing directly to me. Directly into my soul.

I try to pour all my emotions into my voice. I close my eyes and sing the lyrics that I've heard a million times.

"*I lose myself in you. Follow where you lead. All my dreams come true. Everything I need.*"

When I finish, I pass the megaphone to Zak, who is

looking at me with the widest eyes I've ever seen. He looks stunned. Like he just saw a starfish weave a basket.

Guess he didn't expect me to be able to actually sing.

But he can't gawk long because the chorus begins and it's his turn.

The moment he puts the megaphone to his mouth, I have to bite my lips to keep from laughing. He wasn't wrong. He is a *terrible* singer. Like merfolk-passing-by-stop-and-stare terrible.

His voice cracks, he's way off-key, and he keeps reversing the words at the ends of the lines. But as the song goes on, gradually his nerves seem to fade away. The terrified look in his eyes is replaced by an ever-growing smile. Like he gave up trying to be perfect and just decided to go for it.

I have never seen someone enjoy being terrible as much as Zak is right now.

By the time he passes the megaphone back to Zanzia, the gathered crowd is laughing. Not *at* him. *With* him.

His fun is infectious.

When the group song is over, Zanzia and Goby stay on stage to sing a duet. Zak and I float down into the audience to watch them.

"You have an amazing voice," Zak whispers.

I try not to be embarrassed by the compliment. "Thanks."

"Here." Zak unties the cypraeidae shell necklace that hangs around his neck. "The award for the best karaoke singer of the day."

"No, I couldn't."

I try to push it away. Zak wraps his fingers gently around my wrist while he presses the necklace into my palm.

"Please. Keep it," he says. "As a memento."

I want to refuse—it's too real a gift for a fake relationship—but he holds firm. Finally I nod.

He grins and then swims around behind me. I can feel the heat of his fingers as he secures the necklace around my neck.

I press my palm over the speckled cypraeidae shell hanging just below my collarbone. It will be the perfect memento of our time together.

"Come on," I say, not wanting to give myself the chance to think about how soon that time will come to an end, "let's Torpedo again."

Zak grins and takes my hand as we head back to the ride.

NINE

Thursday night

Zak and I didn't make plans for tonight. Which feels weird after spending so much time together all week.

With the game looming big tomorrow, though, I think he wanted to work on his speech. Even though the time is all-too-quickly running out on our fake relationship— which only makes me want to spend even more time with him—I also want to give him the space he needs to get ready.

As I clean up after dinner, I try to picture what he might be doing right now. Working hard, bent over a stack of scribble-filled sheets of kelpaper. Going over every line— every word—again and again. Stressing out.

I wish I could help him.

Wait. I *can* help him.

Just because he didn't ask for help doesn't mean he doesn't need it. Or even want it. Maybe he was just too embarrassed to ask.

I shove the clean seasticks into the drawer and start for my room. The ocean is chilly tonight, and I'll want a sweater for the swim over to his house. I'm just grabbing one off the stack when someone knocks on the front door.

Riatus is closer, so I let him answer.

A few seconds later he calls out, "Coral, it's for you."

For me?

I pull on the sweater as I dash back down. Zak is floating in the front hall, a roll of kelpapers clutched in his hand and a squid ink quill tucked behind his ear. He looks like his normal, happy, smiling self. Almost. There is something lurking in his eyes. A bit of desperation maybe.

"I need help," he says.

"Anything," I answer without hesitation.

And I know that I mean it unequivocally. Zak could ask me to help him rob the Royal Treasury and I would start practicing my lock picking skills.

Not that I currently have any lock picking skills, but I would become an expert.

For Zak, I would anything.

"My speech." He holds up the handful of kelpaper sheets. "I'm running out of time and it's a mess."

The veneer of always-cheerful Zak slips away. He looks miserable, like he wants to swim into a vent worm hole and never come out. That's not all, though. He looks something I never thought I would see Zak Marlin look: scared.

On the karaoke stage he'd looked nervous, definitely. But nothing even close to this.

My insides clench. Every last instinct inside me wants to make it better, to wipe that fear away and replace it with the carefree, confident Zak I've loved for more than four years.

"Come on," I say, turning and starting for the dining room. "We can fix this."

"You kids want some refreshments?" Riatus offers.

"No, thanks," Zak answers.

At the same time, I say, "Kelpberry cupcakes."

Riatus gives me a fake-angry look. He thought I didn't know he had a box of my favorite cupcakes hidden in the cupboard behind the cans of sea peas and tuna stew.

Sorry, bro. Dire circumstances call for tasty reinforcements.

Zak and I settle in next to each other at the big round dining table. He shifts nervously as I take the stack of papers and read over what he's written.

I've given enough speeches on behalf of the environmental club to qualify as a master speechwriter. It only takes me two reads to spot the problem. He makes some really good points, has some powerful lines about teamwork and challenges. The kind of phrases that would work great on a t-shirt. But he goes off on too many tangents that distract from his main points.

The message gets lost.

"Can I?" I reach toward him and point at the quill that's tucked behind his ear.

He gives me a relieved grin. "Of course."

My fingers brush over his golden curls as I grab the quill. I'm too focused on my task to give in to the shiver that races down my spine. I have a job to do.

This time, as I read through the speech, I start marking it up. Deleting repetitive phrases, suggesting stronger word choices, rearranging sentence order to increase their impact.

By the time I'm done, I can barely decipher my own notes. I read through the whole thing, start to finish, to make sure it makes sense.

Finally satisfied, I pull a blank sheet of kelpaper from the bottom of the stack and start rewriting the whole thing with my changes in place. I make a couple more tweaks as I transcribe.

When I'm done, I look up and find Zak taking a bite of cupcake.

"When did Riatus bring those?" I ask.

I glance toward the kitchen and see my brother putting away the large pot he'd used to make dinner.

Zak swallows and smiles. "While you were shredding my speech. You didn't even notice."

I'm a little embarrassed and a lot flattered by the pride I see in Zak's eyes. I only hope the speech lives up to that expectation.

"Well, I *am* a mergirl on a mission." I push the rewritten speech across the table. "Here, try this."

He leans over the papers and starts reading it through.

"I mean out loud," I tell him.

Zak blinks. "Right now?"

"Would you rather practice now, in front of me?" I ask. "Or a stadium full of people?"

I feel bad for reminding him about the crowd, but he needs to be prepared for the situation. If he can't even read the speech to me, how will he ever be able to handle the mob at the game?

He looks momentarily stricken. Then he nods and picks up the speech.

I pull the plate with the remaining kelpberry cupcake toward me, intent on busying myself with the frosting to keep Zak from feeling too self-conscious.

He clears his throat, swallows hard, nods again, and—finally—starts reading.

The moment the speech—the blend of his words and mine—starts flowing from his mouth, I am transfixed. I forget about everything else. My cupcake hangs untouched. I'm sure I look like a whale shark trolling for plankton, mouth hanging open in awe.

I am hooked on every word. And not just because I wrote some of them. Because of the meaning he puts behind the words. His emotion brings them to life.

When he finishes, I reach out and grab his hand. "That was perfect!"

"Thanks." He blushes furiously. "But it was easy because it's you."

"I'm still an audience," I explain. "Tomorrow there will just be a lot more of me."

He shakes his head.

"No, you're different," he says, his voice low and serious. "There's only one Coral."

My heart thuds in my chest like a tsunami crashing into

the shore. Something about the way he said it makes me think he's not just talking about the speech.

I'm being ridiculous—hearing what I want to hear. We're just faking a romance. I can't let myself forget that, not for a second.

But I can't shake the feeling that maybe—just *maybe*—there's something more.

"Then pretend like it's just me," I say softly.

He looks down, and I realize that I'm still holding his hand. My eyes widen as he turns his hand over so that we are palm to palm. Blood is pounding through my veins so hard that I'm sure he can feel my pulse.

His hand gently squeezes mine as he leans closer. "Coral, I—"

Crash!

We both jump apart as a loud noise echoes from the kitchen.

"Sorry!" Riatus calls out. "Everything is fine. Nothing happened."

And like that—*poof!*—the moment is over.

Zak blinks several times, like he's waking up from a dream. A dream I'd like to spend the rest of my life in, please.

But there's no use crying over something that washed away on the tide. Whatever he was about to say is gone, like the words I scratched out of his speech.

Instead, he says, "I-I'd better get home." He flashes me an unusually awkward smile. "Need to be back early to swim you to school."

"Right," I say, trying—and failing—to disguise my disappointment. "Early."

The silence between us is deafening. As Zak gathers up the kelpapers of his speech. As I hand him his squid ink quill. As we swim together to the front door.

I'm afraid he's going to swim away without saying another word. But before he opens the door, he turns back to me.

"Thanks for this." He holds up the rewritten speech. "You made me sound smart."

"You *are* smart," I insist, fighting a blush. "I just gave it a little polish."

"Well, you made me sound smart*er*."

I give him a small smile and wave as he swims off into the night.

When the door closes behind him, I float there staring at the smooth stone surface. I don't want to move. I don't want to do anything to make this moment—this feeling—end.

What just happened? Or, more precisely, what just *almost* happened? What had Zak been about to say?

For a second there, for an instant, it definitely felt like....

No, it's not possible. No way was Zak Marlin—*Zak Marlin!*—about to make some kind of emotional confession.

No. Way.

But maybe....

"Are you sure it's just a game?" Riatus asks from behind me.

I take a deep breath to get my runaway imagination under control before whirling around to face him.

"Of course it is," I tell him.

I'm also telling myself. Because that's the truth. Isn't it?

It's fake. The chances that Zak had been about to kiss me were like a billion to none. Right?

My brother lifts a skeptical eyebrow before turning and swimming away.

I close my eyes and rewind through everything that happened tonight. Zak showing up and wanting my help. Zak telling me I'm different. Zak about to say—or *do*—something serious that my stupid brother had to go and interrupt with his stupid kitchen crash.

My heart does a giant flip-flop.

Maybe Riatus is right. Maybe it's not just a fake relationship. Not anymore.

Maybe, in my quest to protect myself from a broken heart, I've missed the signs that Zak's feelings have changed along the way.

For the first time since this fake relationship started— no, since my crush on Zak crashed into my heart four long years ago—I think that maybe, just maybe, there might be a chance.

For me.

For *us*.

I know one thing for certain: I'll never know if I don't tell him how I feel. The sooner the better.

Not tonight, though. I don't want to distract him from his speech.

After the game tomorrow night. I'll tell Zak how I feel

—how I've always felt—and cross my fingers that he finally feels the same way.

As I swim back upstairs, I can't keep the bubbles of hope from tickling my nose like sparkling gelatin on New Year's Eve.

Tomorrow can't come fast enough.

TEN

Friday night

THE BLEACHERS around the QSA stadium are overflowing. Give Back Week games always draws a big crowd. The whole school turns out, along with a lot of family members and alumni.

So far this season, attendance at regular games has been pretty dismal. Everyone says the team's prospects are grim without Zak to lead them and, if I'm being honest, they might not be wrong. We haven't won a single game yet.

No wonder the stands have been practically empty.

Tonight, though, the stands are as full as they used to be when Zak played. Beyond full. There are merfolk floating anywhere and everywhere they can get a view of the field.

It was supposed to be a surprise, but clearly the secret is out.

Everyone wants to see Zak.

The teams are on the field, warming up. On the far end, the Manatees from Marianus Central are trying to get a seaball past their goalie. On the near end, our Seadragons are swimming in a circle, passing the seaball from player to player. When it gets to this year's captain, Seira, she whirls in a circle and starts passing back the other way.

"I think we're going to win," I say to Zanzia.

She plucks a piece of calamari curry from the tub between us. "That's because you're an optimist."

I shrug. "It doesn't cost anything to think positive."

"You think positive enough for both of us."

I smile and shake my head. Partly because it's true—I do tend to be overly optimistic. What's the harm in hoping for the best? But also because Zanzie isn't anywhere near the sea-is-sinking pessimist that she likes to pretend she is. Beneath the prickly, brightly-colored exterior, she's as much of a softie as I am. Which is just one of the reasons that we're best friends.

"When is Zak's speech?" she asks.

"After the anthem." I point at the hourglass draining away at the far end of the field. "Which is after warmups are over."

As we're watching, Halurus loses his grip on the seaball and sends it spiraling toward the other team's bench. The crowd lets out a collective groan.

Zanzia snorts. "Can't even catch a direct pass."

"Maybe he's nervous?" I suggest.

Even I have to admit that the team isn't exactly full of superstars.

We lost a lot of our best players after last season. Zak

and the other graduating seniors were a once-in-a-generation phenomenon. We only have two Year Twelves this season and one Year Eleven. The rest are all underclassfolk. They can't be expected to live up to the impressive legacy of possibly the greatest team in school history.

It's going to take them a while to get used to playing at this level.

At least that's what I'm telling myself. I have faith.

"I don't know what you said to Zak last night," Zanzie says, not taking her eyes off the field, "but when he came home, he was an entirely different merguy."

I fight to keep from blushing. "I don't know what you mean."

"Before he went to see you, he was on the verge of freaking out," she says. "But after, he was totally calm. Like he's even excited to give his speech."

Zanzia flicks a glance at me, but I quickly turn my attention to selecting my next bite from the bucket.

"I don't know." I shrug as casually as possible. "I just helped him practice."

But maybe she's not wrong. Now that I think about it, Zak did seem way more relaxed on the swim to school this morning. And when we met up after.

He was actually grinning when he said he'd meet me outside the locker room after the game.

Maybe my help really did make a difference.

Rheeeeeeen!

Zanzie claps a startled hand to her chest as the buzzer sounds to signal the end of warmups. My own heart pounds in anticipation as the teams swim to their benches for the opening ceremony.

The countdown to Zak's speech is officially on.

First, though, the Thalassinian royal anthem.

Gracilliara swims out to the center of the field and faces the bleachers, her long black hair flowing behind her, almost all the way to the tip of her tailfin. She draws in a deep breath and then starts belting out the lyrics. As one, the crowd starts to sing along.

Everyone else's eyes are on her and the royal flag that Chromis is swimming around the field, but mine are on the tunnel that leads from the home team locker room. That's where Zak will come out.

I can't help wondering how he feels. Is he nervous? Is he excited? Is he going to look for me in the crowd?

As Gracilliara hits the high last note, the crowd cheers.

She bows and swims off as Coach Psolus swims out onto the field. My blood pounds in my ears.

He holds up his hands to quiet the crowd.

"Thank you, everyone, for coming out to support the team on this special night. We have a special surprise for you tonight." He grins at the merfolk filling the stands. "Though, judging by the crowd, I think the secret is already out."

He laughs as he gestures toward the tunnel.

"Our homecoming guest is none other than former team captain, kingdom all-star, and all-around seaball legend Zak Marlin."

Before he's even finished saying Zak's name the crowd

erupts. Cheering so loudly that the sudden wave probably sets off tsunami warning systems around the world.

"Zak is back from college to give our annual Give Back Game speech. Help me welcome," Coach shouts, "*Zak! Marlin!*"

Zak emerges from the tunnel.

I literally cannot hear myself think. The crowd is going absolutely crazy. If this excitement keeps up, it's going to create a whirlpool around the stadium.

I try to tune all of the madness out and focus on the field.

As I watch Zak swim out to join Coach facing the crowd, I study him, looking for any signs that he's nervous or freaking out. He looks maybe a little embarrassed, but otherwise fine. I let out a small sigh of relief.

The adoration of the crowd is staggering.

For the first time, I really think about what this must be like for him. Not just giving the speech, but also his slice of celebrity. He loves the admiration, of course. Who wouldn't? But maybe—just maybe—he also fears it?

Maybe speaking in front of a crowd isn't the only thing that worries him. Maybe it's speaking in front of *this* crowd. Maybe it's not wanting to let *this* crowd down or tarnish their perfect image of him.

This whole situation makes me realize how much he has to carry on his shoulders. No matter how broad those shoulders are, this has to be overwhelming.

I've been one of the crowd for so long. But now I feel like I'm outside of it. Like I understand the real Zak better after one week of fake dating than years of obsessive observation.

I love him more than ever.

I'm grinning like a lovestruck fool as Coach helplessly tries to get the crowd to quiet down for Zak's speech. Zak floats next to him, smiling so big that most people wouldn't see the shadow of worry in his eyes.

"Holy hammerhead," Zanzia says with an exasperated sigh. "He's loving this, isn't he?"

"A little. But maybe a little anxious, too." I gesture at the bleachers. "Don't you think this is intimidating?"

The crowd seems to have grown even bigger since Coach announced Zak's speech. A flutter of bubble messages must have brought out all the fans who hadn't heard—or didn't believe—the rumors.

Zanzia shrugs. "He's used to it."

That's probably true. But maybe there are some things you can't get used to. Maybe there are some pressures that never get easier.

An assistant coach swims out onto the field and hands Coach a megaphone.

"*Quiet!*"

His shout crashes over the crowd, and after a few more cheers everyone finally calms down.

A girl from somewhere in the visitor's end of the stands shouts, "I love you, Zak!"

Zanzia makes a gagging sound.

I bite my lips to hide a giggle. There's that side of the adoration, too.

"Okay, okay," Coach says, still using the megaphone

even though the crowd has quieted down. "If you can hold it together now, let's hear from Zak."

He hands Zak the megaphone.

Zak smiles and sets it on the ground next to him. The crowd has fallen so silent in anticipation that he doesn't need it.

"Thanks Coach," he says. Then, to the crowd, "And thank you for this crazy welcome. Let's save some of that energy for the team. Because we're going to win this game."

The crowd cheers.

Zak stands there, looking out over the merfolk gathered to watch the game. I'm impressed that he doesn't even have his notes, which means he's going to speak from memory.

As he begins, I cross my fingers and fins for him.

"Four years ago," he says, with just the tiniest quiver in his voice, "I was sitting right there waiting to play my first game."

He points to the team bench.

"I had never been so scared in my entire life." He smiles and coughs out a little laugh. "Well, until now."

The crowd laughs with him and, even from this distance, I can feel him relax. I relax with him.

"What got me through that game," he continues, "was knowing that I wasn't alone. Knowing that I was surrounded by merfolk ready to support me every flick of the way. I had teammates on either side of me, ready to catch the ball that I missed or to screen my defender so I could break away to score."

He looks at the players sitting on the bench and his

affection for every single one of them—even those he's never played with—is obvious.

"I also had the coaches at my back. To teach me and push me to be a better seaball player and a better merman. To keep me afloat when things were bad and to reel me in when things were good."

Coach Psolus looks like he wants to burst with pride.

"And, finally, there were those in front of me." Zak pans his gaze across the stands. "The fans, friends, and family who were there for me no matter what. Whether I was riding the wave of an amazing run or surfing low on an epic losing streak."

He floats there for a second, giving the crowd a chance to absorb his words. Hopefully they get the message about supporting the team, even when they aren't winning.

"Those are the merpeople who matter. The ones behind you." He points to the bench. "The ones at your side." He gestures at the coaches. "And the ones right in front of you."

My breath catches as I swear he looks directly at me.

Which is impossible, of course, because how would he even know where to look. Right?

"The ones who have been there all along," he says. "And who will be with you through thick and thin, ups and downs, now and always."

My heart thuds. It feels as if Zak is speaking directly to me. Only to me.

A warning voice at the back of my mind whispers that he's just giving a good speech. That he's speaking to everyone in attendance. Everyone probably feels that way.

But part of me wonders if—hopes that—he's sending a special message just to me.

The crowd jets up from their seats, clapping and cheering so loudly for Zak that I swear I'm not going to be able to hear anything for a week.

I can't stop smiling, though.

I am so proud of him. He did such a good job. He didn't stumble or stutter or miss a beat. He delivered his speech—*our* speech—like a seasoned pro.

He swims off to join Coach on the bench and the teams take the field.

"Wow, that was really good," Zanzia says.

I glance at her and can tell that she's actually impressed. It takes a lot to impress her.

"Sometimes people surprise you," I say with a grin.

She raises her eyebrows. "Clearly."

I turn back to face the field with my cheeks burning pink. Now that the speech is over and the game is under-way, all I can think about is Zak. About *after* the game. About how I'm finally going to tell him how I feel and maybe—hopefully!—hear that he's starting to feel the same way about me.

My life will never be the same.

ELEVEN

Friday night, later

WITH ONLY SECONDS LEFT, the game is tied at seven. I'm beyond anxious, floating at the edge of my seat. I can feel the same anxious energy from the entire crowd.

Many of them came for Zak's speech. But after hearing his message, they stayed for the team. And the team showed up for them.

This is the best they've played all season.

Our team huddles in tight around Coach, getting their last-minute instructions. Zak floats a little off to the side with Tealia, our team flipper—the player who will tailfin-kick the ball toward the net if it comes down to a last-ditch effort to win.

Tealia is just a Year Ten, and since Zak played in pretty much every game last year, she's barely had any actual game experience. Especially not a high-pressure game like this. I can only imagine how nervous she is right now.

If anyone can quell her nerves and get her ready for the overwhelming situation, it's Zak. As they talk, her body language changes. She slowly morphs from a hermit crab hiding in a shell into one proudly parading it around on the sand.

By the time Coach breaks the huddle, I can tell that she's feeling way more confident.

Zak is a natural-born coach. It's the perfect mix of his skills and passions. If Coach Psolus isn't ready to pass on his whistle by the time Zak graduates college, I bet Zak will start coaching the guppy league.

I have a flash of what our future life could be like. Zak coaching the team and teaching fitness and physical education. Me teaching biology and ocean science and sponsoring the environmental club.

What could be more perfect?

Get a grip, Coral, I warn myself. *You haven't even told him how you feel yet. Don't start planning the wedding.*

The referee signals the end of the time-out and the teams swim back onto the field. They line up facing each other, with our flipper floating a few feet behind our main line.

The other team is bigger and stronger. It's been a battle to advance every yard, and more than a couple of our players have been banged up along the way. But we're faster and we play smarter.

We can win.

I suck in a breath and fight the urge to close my eyes when the ref blows the whistle. I can't look away.

The players on both sides start moving. It's like watching an elaborate dance routine. Both lines kick off, meeting in the middle and grappling for position. Seria receives the ball from Halurus, then passes it quickly to Tealia, who freezes for an instant. Her entire body suspended in time.

"You've got this, Tealia," Zak yells from the bench.

His shout snaps her out of it.

Instead of holding the ball in flipping position, she wraps both arms around it and pushes off with a powerful kick. I watch, jaw-dropped, as she swims fast-as-lighting over the grappling lines. She navigates between the shark-like defenders on the far side, narrowly darting between them as they both dive for her.

Then she's free. A clear shot to the net.

The crowd screams.

I scream.

Even Zanzia screams.

We shout as one, "Go Tealia, go!"

And she does.

In the most beautiful seaball move I've ever seen—and that's saying a lot, since I spent most of the last four years watching Zak play—Tealia twists over and around their goalie. As she shoots past him, she flicks the ball into the net.

The bell sounds.

We win!

If I thought the crowd was going crazy before, I had no

clue. Every sea creature in the kingdom must be able to hear this roar.

I have so much excitement pulsing through my body that I can't sit still. I squirm until I can't contain it. I grab Zanzia into an excited hug.

She hugs me back. Which is pretty much the most excited I've ever seen Zanzia get about sports. Despite having a brother who was the biggest seaball star in school history—or maybe because of that—she's never been too into it. But it's hard not to get excited by this kind of game. Especially when our team comes out on top.

When I release her, she smiles. "I didn't think it was possible to care this much about sports."

"It's easy to get caught up in the emotion," I reply with a laugh.

And I'm not only talking about the game. I know my emotions are extra high right now because of what's going to happen after.

What's going to happen *now*.

Or at least what I *hope* is going to happen. What I haven't allowed myself to think might be an actual possibility until this very moment.

My heart starts thudding faster and faster in my chest. I draw in a deep breath. Talking to Zak will be a disaster if I don't get myself under control.

The crowd swarms the field, surrounding the team and congratulating them. Zanzie and I aren't the only ones excited by the win.

"Okay, I've maxed out my cheerleading energy for the

year," Zanzia says, watching the party on the field. "Are you coming over for dinner?"

I smile at the exuberant celebration. "Definitely. I just have to do one thing first."

Nothing major. Just confessing to her brother that I've loved him for four years and I hope he's starting to have feelings for me too. That's a normal, everyday thing, right?

Maybe I won't tell Zanzia that part. Not yet.

"Cool," she says, turning away from the field. "I'll see you at home."

As Zanzie swims off over the stands, I take a pause to absorb this moment. No matter what happens, this is the end of my secret crush. Where no one except my too-observant brother and my devious best friend knows how I feel about Zak.

Everything is going to change.

Hopefully it's a change for the better. Hopefully Zak feels the same way and we can figure out the next part together.

I'm not a fool, though. I know there's a risk that my confession will change things for the worse. But I trust Zak enough to believe that even if it's not the outcome I want, he won't let it affect my relationship with his family.

I trust him with everything.

Even my heart.

By the time I'm done meditating on what I'm about to do, the team has left the field and the crowd is finally starting to dissipate. I scan the field, looking for Zak's blond head.

When I don't see him, I know it's time to go. It's time to

meet him at the end of the locker room tunnel. It's time to confess my feelings.

It's time to face my future—for good or for bad.

I push up from the bleachers and head for our designated meeting spot.

The area around the end of the tunnel is deserted. Zak must be in the locker room with the team. He'll be here when they're done.

I just have to wait.

Did I mention that patience is not one of my virtues? My mind races and I can't stop cycling through a rainbow of emotions.

I'm so excited for the team's win. They've had a lot of doubters this year, and they just proved everyone wrong in a single epic game. And thanks to Zak's speech, they had half the kingdom in the stands, cheering them on.

The stands are going to be packed for the rest of the season.

I'm also feeling proud of Zak. He helped the flipper a lot this week, and I know he felt amazing when she scored the winning goal.

That's probably where he is, helping Tealia celebrate.

But the other feeling tickling at my thoughts is terror. Not just because I'm afraid of what Zak's reaction to my confession will be—like I said, whatever it is I think we'll be able to keep being friends—but because I'm finally about to reveal this secret I've been keeping for so long.

Finally giving voice to my deepest and most private dream.

Finally knowing the answer to the question I've never had the courage to ask.

That's enough to terrify the bravest mergirl.

But I'm trying not to focus on the fear. I'm trying to think positive. I'm trying to be calm. Being an emotional basketcase won't make this any easier or any better.

I check the tunnel again.

I fidget with my hair—which is beyond any possibility of control, as always.

I smooth down the hem of my tankini top.

I decide that I should wait on the other side of the tunnel. No, the other side.

By the time I've swum back and forth across the narrow opening several times I'm starting to worry. It feels like forever since the game ended. It's not like Zak to be *this* late. Maybe I got it wrong. Maybe I was supposed to meet him on the field. Maybe he's out there waiting for me right now, just as worried about me as I am about him.

Rather than float here stewing until I lose my mind, I decide to go check.

As soon as I round the end of the stands I see him. Floating in front of the home team bench.

I smile with both relief and awkward self-condemnation.

"Way to get it wrong," I whisper to myself.

I kick out onto the field. I open my mouth, ready to call out to him—to say something self-effacing about how I'm such a loser I can't even remember where we're supposed to meet—but I stop when I see that Zak isn't alone.

Not only isn't he alone, but he isn't alone...*with Angel.*

He's so not alone with Angel that they have their arms wrapped around each other.

In an instant, my every dream dissolves like a sandcastle in a storm. Tiny flecks of hope and heart swirling around in the surf, at the mercy of the current.

How could I have been so wrong?

No, how could I have been so *stupid?*

I smack a hand over my mouth before the sound that is bubbling up from my chest can burst out.

My only thought is escape. I whirl around and race back toward the tunnel. I'm so desperate to get away that I don't see the other merperson in the tunnel until it's too late.

"Oooof!" Chromis exclaims as the force of my speed knocks him into the tunnel wall.

"Sorry," I gasp, barely containing the sobs that are building up inside. "I'm...s-sorry."

He straightens his glasses. "Coral. You're..."

He frowns at me.

I bite my lips to keep from saying anything.

"You're crying," he observes very matter-of-factly.

I can't handle it. I can't even speak or everything will gush out of me and I won't be able to stop.

I shake my head—a mix of apology and denial—before turning and continuing my flight.

As I sprint for home, a thousand thoughts race through my mind. Flashes of memory from the past few days. Rewinding and reliving every little moment, looking for clues and cues.

At the core of it all is the realization that I totally set myself up for this exact heartbreak. I let myself get invested in this fake relationship. I let myself dare to believe it could be more, when all along I knew that Zak's goal was to get Angel back. That's the whole reason we did this.

I'm just the crush-blind fool who forgot that inconvenient fact.

Well, the plan worked. Zak got what he wanted, and my heart got exactly what it deserved.

That doesn't make it any less painful. In fact, it might make it worse. My heart has been shattered into infinite pieces. I'm sure my eyes have never glittered so bright with tears.

As I swim for home as fast as my fins will take me, desperate for the solitude of my room and the comfort of my bed, I decide that the only thing that might make this even the tiniest bit bearable would be a bottomless bowl of plumaria pudding. And even that would only dull the sharpest edges of the pain.

TWELVE

Friday night, even later

By some miracle, I don't run into anyone on the swim home and the house is empty when I get there. I can't face anyone right now. I especially can't face Riatus. I'm not prepared to deal with his I-warned-you-about-this face.

He won't mean to give me that look, but he won't be able to help it.

And, really, I can't exactly blame him. He was right.

But just because he's not here right now doesn't mean I'm in the clear. He could get home at any time. I need to lock myself away before he does. And I will need provisions.

I do a quick swim-by in the kitchen, grab a box of caramel cookies and a jar of fudge cream, and then sprint straight for my room.

Moments later, I'm snuggled under the covers, trying to pretend like nothing from the last week ever happened.

Trying to forget all of those moments that I was savoring only a short time ago. Starting from the one when I ran into Zak outside the school last Friday.

It had all been leading to this.

If only I had listened to my gut. If only I had listened to Riatus.

If only I could perform a mer-powered memory wipe on myself.

I dig a cookie through the fudge cream and then stuff it into my mouth.

Deep down inside, I'm really just mad at myself. I went into this with eyes wide open. I knew that Zak wanted to get Angel back, that they probably *would* get back together, considering their history.

Somewhere along the way I forgot that inconvenient truth.

I grab another cookie out of the box.

Why am I so upset about something as inevitable as the tide? I knew this was coming, so shouldn't I be able to deal?

But I know the answer.

Over the last few days, I've gotten a taste of what a real relationship with Zak would be like. How it would feel to know that I would get to see and talk to and even touch him whenever I wanted. No more furtive glances or secret stalking.

It felt good. It felt way too good.

And more than that, I got to know Zak better than I thought I already did. Every new thing I learned about him only made me love him more.

Now, having experienced something beyond my wildest

dreams and knowing that I'll never have that again makes it a million times worse.

I shove one more fudge-covered cookie into my mouth and then pull the covers tighter over my head. I let the tears flow. There's no point in fighting them anyway.

My blood pounds loudly in my ears. Maybe my heart is so broken that it's actually *broken*.

But when I pull back the covers to draw some heart-calming breaths, the noise is even louder. *Thud, thud, thud.* A pounding coming from downstairs.

Someone is at the front door.

It wouldn't be Riatus because, well, he wouldn't knock.

Which can only mean that it's Chromis. I shouldn't have swum away after I knocked him into the wall. Obviously I shouldn't have knocked him into the wall either, but it wasn't like I was in full—or even partial—control of myself at that moment.

He's probably worried about me. He should be, too, and I feel bad for that.

But I'm nowhere near ready to face him right now. I'm nowhere near ready to face *anyone* right now. I can't exactly explain why I'm a sobbing mess while I'm, you know, a sobbing mess.

Plus, I couldn't handle the pity.

I'll send Chromis a bubble message later.

I go back under the covers and dig around for the cookie box, fully expecting him to go away. But the pounding doesn't stop.

I never knew he was so persistent.

Even the grinding crunch of chewing cookies can't drown out the pounding.

Finally I can't stand it anymore. I fling back the covers, wipe the cookie crumbs away, and swim downstairs. No amount of wiping will disguise my tear-glittered eyes, but he already knows I was crying.

I'll show Chromis that I'm fine, apologize for shoving him into a wall, and be back under the covers with my cookies in no time.

Only when I pull open the door, it's not sweet-but-awkward Chromis floating outside.

"Zak?"

I squeeze my eyes shut and pray to Poseidon and every sea nymph he ever sired that when I open them again the glittery signs of my tears will be gone.

It's a faint hope, but hey, I'm desperate.

When I open my eyes, I flash the biggest, brightest smile I can manage. Hopefully that will distract him from my sparkling eyes.

"Zak, hi, what's up?" I say, buying myself time to think of something clever. "Oh, right, we were supposed to meet, huh?"

He frowns a little, confused by my tactic maybe. Good. Stay confused.

"I ran into Chromis," he says.

"That poor merguy," I interject. "I ran into him too. Hard. Kind of knocked him into a wall."

I laugh way too loud for it to sound remotely natural. *Get. A. Grip.*

I clench my hands into fists, digging my nails into my palms as a reminder to keep my composure. Whatever it takes, I can't let Zak know how much this hurts. I can't let him see that I'm falling apart inside.

It's not his fault that I let myself start to believe our fake relationship was real.

"Yeah, he told me." Zak gives me a nervous smile. "He said you looked upset."

"Upset? Who, me?"

I wave my hand at him in a dismissive gesture. Only I forget that it's clenched in a fist, so it looks like I'm shadow-boxing with him. I unclench my fist and press the hand to my chest.

"No, really," I insist. "I'm fine."

He looks skeptical. Or maybe scared that I'm going to punch him in the nose.

I try to smile even bigger. "It's all good."

I'm holding on by a fragile thread. I blink rapidly as I add a silent plea that he buys my blatant lie and swims away before I lose all control of my emotions.

"You don't seem fine," he says.

"Really, I am," I say, as if repeating it enough might make it true. Maybe he needs a more explicit message. "I just think it's time to end the show."

He frowns. "What show?"

"Us," I tell him. "Our *relationship*."

"End it?" he echoes. "Why?"

"You got what you wanted," I tell him.

"What I wanted?"

My blood pounds louder in my ears. Is he really going to make me say it? Well, if it gets him off my doorstep faster, then I'll spell it out. Even if it feels like I'm cutting my heart out with a rusty fillet knife.

"Angel. I saw you two after the game." I force a really awkward giggle. "You got her back."

"It's not like that."

"No, it's fine." There's that dang word again. *Fine.* It might be the worst word in the English language. "You got what you wanted, Zak. The perfect couple is a couple once more. Your mom will be thrilled."

"I'm sorry you saw that, but—"

I cut him off. "Seriously, Zak."

My tone is intentionally a little harsh. I can't take it anymore. If he doesn't stop, I won't be able to hold it together. And holding it together is all I have right now.

"It's all fi—" I refuse to say that word ever again. "Fabulous. It's great. This is what we talked about. This was the whole reason for our fake relationship."

"It wasn't—"

"To be honest, faking this relationship has been exhausting." I drift to the left and lean myself up against the doorway.

"It has?"

I will *not* notice the cute little confused wrinkle that just appeared between his brows. I will *not* add that to the list of things I love about him.

But I *will* notice that he drifts back a little bit.

"Totally," I say with a laugh, grateful that I seem to have

found a way to push him away. I just have to push a little harder. "I'm relieved that it's over. It's one less thing that I have to worry about."

He opens his mouth to say something more. Can he seriously not tell that I don't want to talk this out? We agreed to end this with a clean break. He needs to let it be clean.

"Zak. It's okay." I release a tiny bit of control, just enough to give him a hint of how much this whole conversation hurts. Hopefully enough to convince him to drop it. "Please. Go."

I reach for the door and start to close it.

He doesn't leave. But he doesn't say anything more. He just floats there, looking more confused than ever and, right now, I can't care. I can't worry about his feelings when mine are on the verge of bursting out of me like hot water from a deep-sea thermal vent.

As I slide the door closed, I can't help adding, "Congrats on helping the team win."

The instant the door clicks shut, I lose it. The tears pound out of me in gut-wracking sobs. All control is gone. I've never cried so hard in my life. My lungs draw in great gasping breaths, as if desperately trying to draw in enough water to wash away my pain.

I need to get upstairs and under the covers before Riatus gets home. I can't face his questions tonight. I can't face anything.

It's going to take a lot more than sugary treats to get through this. If I even can.

Maybe, for the rest of my life, I'm going to have a Zakshaped hole in my heart. Maybe that's the price I have to pay for loving him and letting myself believe that he might ever love me that way too.

Tomorrow, it might seem like a bargain.

Right now, that price feels way too high.

THIRTEEN

Saturday morning

A MESSAGE BUBBLE wakes me up the next morning, floating in through my open window and landing on my bedside table with a soft plop.

I should ignore it, but I can't resist. I roll over and pry one eyeball open. Not that I have to look to know who sent it.

It's the fourth one so far.

The moment I see it's from Zak, I flick my hand and send it sailing back out. It will get returned to him, marked undelivered and unopened. Just like the first three messages he sent, starting at dawn.

I just can't right now.

This wasn't the best night's sleep I've ever had. In fact, it was probably the worst.

Before this, the worst was the one right after Riatus had

to go away for a year. I was so nervous for him, so worried about what might happen and when I might see my big brother again. I kept turning it over and over in my mind, and when I did fall asleep, I had nightmares about him being fed to a Great White.

Last night was worse.

I got maybe an hour of fitful sleep. Big maybe.

My mind had only *just* calmed down enough to drift away again when the latest message bubble arrived. There went my chance of *any* sleep.

Thanks a lot.

It's not so much that I'm mad at Zak. How could I be? I mean, he was completely honest about what he wanted from the fake relationship.

Not me. I was the one who kept her feelings to herself.

Really, I'm just mad at myself for letting those feelings get involved as much as they did. I knew it would be bad. I told myself to lock them away, to protect my heart at all costs. But I couldn't keep hope from slipping in through the cracks.

I have only myself to blame.

As if moping around is going to change anything. I should snap out of it. I knew this was going to happen, so why am I so utterly devastated over it?

Because a broken heart doesn't care who's to blame. It's still broken.

No matter how much I try to tell myself to stop acting like my world imploded, I can't hold back the pain.

There's no use pretending that I'm going to get any more sleep than I've already gotten. Even with a full eight hours, I would still be floating through today like a zombiefish. Might as well face the day.

I fling back my covers and start for the door. Maybe some extra-sugary overnight groats will make me feel better. I think we have some maple candy hidden in the back of a cupboard.

Riatus is already in the kitchen, making his breakfast and packing his lunch for the day. I hesitate at the door, wondering if I'm ready to face him.

It's not like it will get any easier.

He glances over his shoulder as I float into the room. One look at my face—probably a mix of red-eyed puffiness and don't-even-ask glare—and his face falls. He looks like I punched him in the stomach.

I shake my head once, hard, begging him not to push the subject. He frowns but reluctantly turns his attention back to his food.

For some reason, that makes me feel even worse.

Shaking off the fresh pain, I swim to his side and reach over him to get my groats out of the cupboard. He silently hands me a bowl and a spoon.

"Thanks," I mumble.

As I'm pouring my groats, another message bubble floats in, making its way across the kitchen toward me. I don't even look. I just reach over and flick it back the way it came.

I try to go back to making my breakfast, but I can feel Riatus looking at me.

"Don't," I warn.

He spins to face me. "I didn't say a word."

"Good."

"But if I was going to," he continues, "I would ask if you want to talk about it."

My hand grips the jar so tightly my knuckles start to turn white.

"I can't," I whisper. "Not yet."

When I look up, the sympathetic look he gives me only shatters my battered heart even more. I could have handled the I-told-you-so look. I was expecting that. I was prepared for it.

But this? It only reaffirms how bad I feel.

Maybe I should forget about breakfast. I'm not sure I even feel up to eating. Although those maple candies might make me feel a teeny-tiny bit better.

Maybe I'll just take it up to my room.

I'm still deciding what to do about breakfast when there's a knock on the door.

My eyes immediately dart to Riatus, who is staring at me. I get the feeling he's been staring at me the whole time.

"Could you—"

"I don't want to get in the middle of it," he says before I can ask.

I bite my lips to keep the tears from coming back. I know he's trying to help, trying to force me to face my problems instead of hiding from them. But I can't. Not yet. I need to hide a little longer.

My desperation must show because his expression softens.

"Please," I beg, trying to win him over.

Finally, he nods.

I heave out a huge sigh of relief as Riatus swims to the front door and I float into the corner of the kitchen, so I'll be out of sight from the door. Out of sight from Zak.

I'm holding my breath when I hear Riatus say, "Zanzia, hey."

Sugar-covered starfish.

Zanzia's almost worse. She's my best friend. She will see straight through any I-totally-don't-care facade that I might be able to present to her brother.

I press myself deeper into the corner.

Riatus tries to keep her out. "If you're looking for Coral—"

"Nice try, Ri-Ri," Zanzia says, cutting him off mid-excuse. "I know she's here."

There is nowhere to hide. Maybe if I make myself as flat as possible, I'll blend into the walls. And maybe one day dragon eels will breathe fire.

From the moment Zanzia swims into the kitchen, it only takes her an instant to spot me. I sag in a mix of relief and defeat. One look at me—still in my pajama top, eyes red and swollen, hair a wild mess, hiding in the corner—and she shakes her head.

"You look terrible."

I force out an awkward laugh. "Thanks."

From the corner of my eye, I see Riatus swim by. He hovers in the doorway for a second, as if asking if I want him to intervene. When I ignore him, he swims off, probably heading to his room in the back of the house. I'm sure he wants to be as far away from this as possible.

His door clicks softly shut.

Zanzia crosses her arms over her chest. "Wanna tell me what happened?"

I manage something like a cross between a shrug and a no.

"Well, you're going to," she says. "Because my brother won't say a word."

With a heavy sigh, I swim over to the table and float into the nearest seat. Once Zanzie is on the scent of something, there's no stopping her. If I want any peace, I'll have to talk.

She takes the seat across from me.

"It ended," I say. "What's to tell?"

"Bullshark."

A half-smile breaks my grim mood. Not only does Zanzia have the most colorful hair, she has the most colorful language of anyone I know.

"There's more to it than that." She gestures at me. "You look like something that a hurricane dragged to shore."

I can't disagree.

"And the only merperson I know who looks worse," she says, leaning back into her chair, "is Zak."

In a strange way, that makes me feel both better and worse. Better, because it means that I'm not alone in feeling bad about how this thing ended. Worse, because despite how broken my heart is right now, I still care about him and don't want him in any kind of pain.

Although, to be honest, I don't know why he would be so upset. He got what he wanted. He's back with Angel. He should be thrilled.

Maybe it's because I won't answer his bubble messages.

"You broke his heart, Coral."

Of all the things Zanzia could possibly say, that is the most shocking. And the most ridiculous. She knew the truth about our fake relationship. She knew that Zak was only doing it to get Angel back.

She can't actually believe what Zak is the heartbroken one.

"It wasn't real, Zanzie," I remind her. "For either of us."

It was supposed to be easy. It was supposed to help Zak and, if I'm being honest, give me a taste of what being his girlfriend would be like. That shouldn't have been devastating. To either of us.

The only reason my heart is broken is because I let myself believe that maybe it could be something more than pretend.

Zanzia leans forward over the table. "Try telling him that."

She seems so serious that I feel a tiny bubble of hope tickle at my chest.

No, no, no. I mentally reach in and pop that hope bubble before it can grow any bigger. I let my hopes get too big once, and look what happened. I won't let them do it again. I'm not sure my heart would survive.

"Fine, don't believe me," Zanzia says, as if she's done with the whole situation.

Knowing her, it's not over, but she's not going to push me right now.

Instead, she asks, "What time are we meeting at the theatre?"

The theatre?

Oh right, I totally forgot about the cabaret. I've been so lost in my own drama that it slipped my mind.

Or maybe I just wanted it to slip my mind. It's Zanzia's big triumph, so I know Zak will be there. I can't face him right now.

I don't know when I will be able to.

I know this makes me literally the worst best friend in all the oceans, but I just can't.

"You don't really need me, do you?" I cross my fingers that she'll let me off the hook. "You've got Goby. Plus, you could run the show in your sleep."

She shakes her head, clearly disappointed in me. "That's not the point."

I know it isn't. The point is she's my best friend and I should be there to support her.

But right now, my insides feel too raw. To face Zak. To face the school. To face anyone.

"I'm sorry," I whisper.

Zanzia stares at me for a long time, like she's trying to see inside my mind. I'm not sure how much longer I can hold it together under her scrutiny.

"You're wrong," she finally says. "About Zak. About what he wanted from your fake relationship."

She pushes up from the table.

"Before you make a mistake that you'll both regret for a really long time," she says, "you should ask him if it was ever about Angel."

Zanzia turns and swims away. I bite my lips to keep a fresh burst of tears from pouring out. She's my best friend and I love her more than anyone who isn't family, but she's wrong about this. It was only ever make-believe.

When I push up from the table, I notice Riatus lurking in the doorway.

He has that I-know-I'm-not-your-dad-but…look on his face. I can't handle it right now.

"Don't say it," I warn. "I already know I'm a terrible friend."

Before he can say anything to make me feel worse—if that's even possible at the moment—I decide to abandon my breakfast altogether and head upstairs. Maybe another hour or twelve under the covers will make things hurt less.

Or maybe it will just make things less recent.

Either outcome is bound to be better than how I feel right now.

FOURTEEN

Saturday afternoon

HIDING under the covers definitely isn't working. I'm not feeling any better, the pain doesn't seem to be moving any further away, and it's definitely hot and harder to breathe in here.

But I'm sticking it out. It's only been a few hours. I've got to give it at least a few days. Maybe, eventually, it will work.

"Knock, knock."

I groan at the sound of my brother's voice. He usually avoids my room like a jellyfish swarm. Like there are some mystical female protection spells surrounding my personal space.

Let me tell you. If I could cast a protection spell around myself right now, I would have already done it. I would have surrounded myself with an impenetrable wall of ice and field of electric eels as an extra deterrent.

I've heard rumors about a powerful sea-witch who lives in the Antillenes. I'm sure she would take pity on my poor broken heart and grant me a little free magic.

"Coral?" Riatus asks softly.

He sounds worried.

I sigh heavily into my pillow. *Don't worry, big brother, I haven't cried myself into a coma. Yet.*

He doesn't get the telepathic message. "Are you—"

I fling back the useless covers. They aren't going to protect me from Riatus any more than they're protecting me from my heartache.

Sitting up in bed, I blink in the bright light. I've been under so long I thought for sure it would be midnight outside.

Riatus hovers outside my open door, floating just beyond the barrier of my would-be spell. I make a mental note to go looking for that sea-witch.

"I'm fine," I tell him.

His eyebrows shoot surface high. Clearly he believes that almost as much as I do.

But apparently my response makes him bold because he gives his navy blue tailfin a flick and swims to my bedside. He stops with another flick, floating down to rest on the edge of my bed.

Oh no. He's got that I'm-going-to-act-like-the-grown-up-here look on his face.

I grab for the covers, but he's sitting on them. When I

give them a tug he just scowls at me. He's not about to let me hide from whatever he's going to say.

I'm one-thousand-percent sure I won't like it.

"This isn't like you," he says.

He stares down at his hands.

He used to be uncomfortable playing the co-guardian role he's had to assume. Over the years, he's gotten better at it. But he still doesn't love it. He's torn between being the protective big brother and the father figure we *both* needed.

I give up trying to sink back under the covers and take pity on him.

"What do you mean?" I ask.

He looks up at me. "You don't usually give up on a problem."

"I've never had one like this before."

Meaning I've never had one that hurt this much before. This is uncharted waters. I've never felt so lost at sea.

"You're stronger than this," Riatus insists. "I know it probably doesn't feel like it right now, but you will survive. Someday, this will be a distant memory. You will be stronger still for having gone through the heartbreak."

He says the last words in such a soft voice that my heart breaks all over again. What is it about tender sympathy that makes me feel even worse?

I swear, if he takes my hand or pats my shoulder, I'm going to shatter.

But just when I think that he's said all he came in here to say, he clears his throat and says, "And when you've pushed the pain aside…"

He pauses, which he only does before he says something I'm really not going to like, and I brace myself.

"…you will be mad at yourself for missing out on this important night."

I groan. There it is. The massive fish hook I didn't see lurking behind the enticing morsel of bait.

"You will be mad at yourself," he continues, as if I haven't flung myself back onto my bed and thrown my arm over my eyes, "for letting down your friend."

I want to say something smart. Or snarky. Or sarcastic and dismissive that says you're-wrong-and-I-can't-hear-you-anymore-*nanananananaaaaa*.

But I can't think of even the lamest comeback.

Dang it. I know what that means.

He's right.

Zanzia is one of the most important people in my life—right after my mom and the lunkhead sitting on the edge of my bed right now—and tonight is important to her. She wants me there. Whether she actually needs me or not is beside the point. If the situation were reversed, she would be floating at my side, heartache or no.

That's what best friends do.

No matter how much I love Zak or how much the sudden end of something that never really existed in the first place hurts right now, Zanzia will always be my best friend. I have to behave like I'm hers.

And as much as it pains me to agree with Riatus—like, ever—I know that he's also right about me. I am still the same strong mergirl I was *before* I saw Zak and Angel on the seaball field yesterday. Only today I'm stronger.

Tomorrow, I'll be stronger again.

That which feels unbearable today will strengthen me tomorrow. I think I read that somewhere. And I might as well start acting like tomorrow is already here.

In a fit of determination, I sit up and flip back the rest of my covers so I can kick out of bed. Or I at least *try* to flip back my covers.

"Riatus, could you—?"

I tug at the bedding. It takes him a second to get the meaning. When he does, he floats up, off my bed and out of my way. Kicking out of my cocoon, I swim over to my desk and start composing a bubble message.

"What are you doing?" Riatus asks.

"I'm telling my backup date to meet me at seven."

Just because I'm going to the cabaret without Zak, doesn't mean I have to go alone.

I don't have to look up to know Riatus is frowning. I can feel it in the water.

"You have a backup date?"

I finish the message and send it on its way. Then I turn to face my brother.

"A mergirl always needs a plan B."

Riatus stares at me for several seconds, like I'm an alien fish species. Then, with a shake of his head, he smiles. To my utter shock, I smile back. I'm amazed that I still can.

In a fit of unexpected joy, I kick away from my desk and wrap my arms around him in a tight hug.

"Thank you," I whisper. "For always nudging me in the right direction."

He hugs me back—a little awkwardly, because hugging

isn't exactly his favorite pastime. I hold onto him for a few seconds more, gathering as much strength from him as I can, before I finally let him go.

He smiles and, I swear, there is the slightest glitter in his eyes. But before either of us starts bawling—though I'm not sure I have any tears left to cry—he pushes up and away. As he swims for the door, I head to my closet.

He pauses on his way out.

"For what it's worth," he says, looking back over his shoulder, "it didn't look fake to me."

I ignore the sharp twinge in my chest. "It just means we did a good job of acting."

He shrugs. "You might want to ask him whether it was just *acting*."

That bubble of hope threatens to reappear in my chest. I reach in and swiftly pop it. My days of hoping for something to be true are over. Just call me Reality Only girl from now on.

"Thanks, but I've taken just about as much brotherly advice as I can in a day." I flash him an exaggerated grin.

He shakes his head and then swims off into the house.

Turning back to my closet, I take a deep breath. The last eighteen hours have been painful enough to last a lifetime. I'm not going to let my heart get any more broken than it already is.

Pushing the pain and heartache into a deep corner of my mind, I focus on getting ready for tonight. My best friend needs me, and I refuse to let her down.

We will make this the best fundraising cabaret the merworld has ever seen.

And tomorrow, everything will be one day closer to better.

FIFTEEN

Saturday evening

I'm a little nervous as I swim up to the theatre. My hands shake and I'm working hard to quiet the worried voices in my head. I've never had a second of doubt in all of my friendship with Zanzia. But we've never faced a situation like this. I've never bailed on her before.

Zanzia has every right to be mad at me. In that moment earlier, I cared more about my heartache over a fake relationship than about our real friendship.

I wouldn't be surprised if she told me to go swim into a hole.

But I have to try.

I know she'll be in the back, getting everything ready. So I swim through the auditorium—waving at Goby, who is carefully setting programs on every seat—over the stage, and into the backstage space.

Zanzie is floating over a table covered in brightly colored sea fans. I bite back a laugh at the thought that she *is* a brightly colored sea fan. Her hair is now practically an entire rainbow.

She's going to run out of colors soon.

It's still early enough that there isn't any other activity behind the scenes yet. No one to call out my name or draw attention to my presence. Zanzie will never know I'm here unless I say something.

Part of me wants to turn around and swim home. But a bigger part of me wants to stay and make things right.

When I can't stand to keep floating there in awkward silence, I swim in a little closer. I take a deep breath and then let it out. No point in flipping around the bush or drawing this out any longer.

"I'm sorry," I say.

They are maybe the two hardest words I've ever had to say in my life. But they are also the two important. Fixing this with Zanzie is unbelievably crucial.

I brace myself for the dressing down I totally deserve.

Zanzia twists around and stares at me for several long, torturous seconds. My heart thuds and my palms itch. The longer she stares, the more I worry that I've actually broken our friendship for good.

I can't read anything in her bright green eyes. I fight the urge to close my own against her incoming judgment.

Finally, when I just about can't bear it anymore, she shakes her head.

"Will you *please*—" She gestures at the table. "—help

me count these lobster-loving sea fans? I keep losing track and having to start over."

My face explodes into the biggest grin of my life.

"Any opportunity to use my math skills," I tell her.

Relief floods my body as I join her at the table. She's smiling too. Maybe she was just as worried about us as I was.

I should have known. A friendship like ours can't be broken by something as temporary as heartbreak.

"You didn't have to apologize," she says, starting her count again. "Showing up is what mattered."

I start counting from the other end of the table.

"I did," I insist. "You didn't have to accept my apology."

She groans as she loses count and moves back to the start.

"I did," she says. "You're my best friend."

I'm about to say, *And you're mine*, when she adds, "Who would I talk to at lunch if I iced you out?"

I laugh out loud, careful not to lose track of my sea fans.

We're both relieved that I came to my senses. And just like that, everything is back to normal. Like it never happened.

This gives me hope that maybe—someday—I'll be able to get back to normal with Zak, too.

For the next two hours, we flick around like dartfish, getting every detail ready for the show. Goby takes care of making sure the performers are all ready. A few other volunteers show up to help move the scenery into place, hang the bioluminescent lighting, and prep the concessions booth.

By the time Zanzie and I are hanging up the costumes for the final number, I'm half-exhausted. Which only makes me feel worse for almost bailing on her. She probably *could* have gotten it all done without me, but barely.

"Can you make sure the turret flutes are on their stands?" Zanzia hangs the last scallop cape on the garment rack. "I need to go take care of something."

"No problem."

I brush my hands over the mother-of-pearl sequins on the bodice of the last costume and then head for the offstage right staging area. The turret flutes are there, but they're still in their boxes.

There are twenty-four flutes to set out. I start opening the boxes, carefully setting each instrument on the corresponding stand. Turret flute music is one of my favorite sounds. I can't wait to hear what the school orchestra performs this year.

I have just opened the last box when I sense movement behind me.

"I'm almost done here," I tell Zanzia. "Should I lay out the first act finale props next?"

There's a long pause. Then, "Coral, we need to talk."

My entire body freezes at the sound of Zak's voice. My heart pounds like a drum and I can barely breathe.

I only just barely managed to swim through my feelings enough to come help my best friend on her big night. My emotions are nowhere near stable enough for this.

Was it too much to ask for a little time to recover?

Without responding to him, I finish taking the last flute

out of the box, my hands trembling as I set it on the stand. Maybe if I take long enough, he'll get the hint. Maybe he'll swim away. Maybe he'll—

"Coral—"

"I can't," I whisper.

I'm not sure *what* I can't. But I just *can't*. Can't turn around. Can't talk to him. Can't listen to him. Can't think about him any more. Can't stop helping Zanzia set up for the show because if I stop moving then I won't be able to hide from my carefully-contained feelings any longer.

"Coral," he tries again.

Something inside me breaks.

"No. I *can't!*" I whirl around to face him, fighting to contain my emotions. "The curtain goes up in less than twenty minutes, and there is still a mountain of work to do. There isn't time."

I swim away from him, heading for the first act finale props table. Only my perpetual movement keeps my body from shaking uncontrollably. I open up the box of mirrors and start laying them out on the places marked on the table.

Clearly not getting the hint, Zak follows me. He grabs the box of forks and starts setting them next to my mirrors.

That kind of unconditional help would normally make me fall even harder for him. But that was the old Coral. The new Coral has a heart of stone and won't be softened just because he starts helping without being asked. No she won't. Not. At. All.

"You didn't answer any of my message bubbles," he says.

He's caught up with me, like it became a race to see who

can place their props fastest. But I'm not a competitive person. Maybe that's why I've never done sports.

I maintain my steady pace while making sure my arm doesn't brush against his.

"There isn't anything more to say," I tell him.

Zak doesn't look up. "You didn't even read them."

No, no, no. My heart will *not* twinge at the hint of sadness in his voice. My heart needs to learn how to protect itself.

I concentrate on my task, making sure each mirror is in the perfect place. I don't want any of the dance team members to miss their prop grab during the quick change.

Plus, focusing on my task helps keep the tears away.

But it's a precarious hold.

One that shatters when he starts to say, "You should know—"

"I can't, okay?!" I shout. "I can't handle this right now."

Zak blinks, stunned by my outburst. Good. I know this behavior is totally out of character for me. Hopefully that shows him how much I mean what I'm saying.

"You have no idea how it feels." I swipe at my eyes. The tears are coming now, and I won't be able to stop them. "You have no idea how *I* feel."

An almost deranged laugh bursts out of me. A voice in the back of my mind begs me not to say what I'm about to say, but I can't keep it in any longer. The dam has burst and the water is flooding everywhere.

"I have loved you for *so* long, and it is taking every single ounce of strength I have to hold myself together right now," I half-growl, half-gasp. "And I *have* to hold myself together right now because Zanzia needs me."

Zak stares at me, unblinking. I have no idea what's going through his mind. I don't even know what's going through *my* mind. Not really.

And for the first time in years, I don't want to know what he's thinking. I'd rather not. I have a feeling I wouldn't like it anyway.

"So please," I beg. "If you care about me *at all*, please stop."

He keeps staring at me. For several long seconds—it feels like hours—the only sound is my ragged breath and the scrape of Goby and a pair of volunteers moving the set pieces for the first act into place.

I watch as a rainbow of emotions plays across Zak's face. I see the shock and confusion and realization and, finally, understanding of what I'm saying—what I'm confessing to —process in a cascading reaction.

He opens his mouth.

I brace myself.

Then, without saying a word, he turns and swims away.

I stare after him for a long time, not sure how to feel. Relieved? Disappointed? Angry? Everything? That's what I wanted, right? For him to leave me alone.

Well, he did. I told him I'd been in love with him for years, and he left.

I should be thrilled, but all I feel is empty.

Which is good. Empty is good. I have work to do. The show must go on, right? And it's not going to go on without my help.

I turn back to the table and continue the methodical work of laying forks next to mirrors. I can indulge in my emotions later. For now, I have a job and I'm going to do it to the best of my ability.

I can continue my breakdown later.

SIXTEEN

Saturday evening, later

THE NEXT TWENTY minutes are a blur of non-stop activity.
I definitely worry that Zanzie is gonna lose it when the lionfish from the opening act escapes and starts tearing through
the big finale costume rack just minutes before the curtain
time. I really would have thought that a trio of lionfish
tamers could keep their fish under control, but apparently
not.

"Go, get changed," I tell her. "Goby and I can
handle it."

Goby nods. "We've got this."

The sneaky little critter is determined to maintain his
freedom. We manage to recapture the lionfish and get him
back into his bubble carrier just as Zanzia returns in a
sequined top that matches the magenta shade in her

rainbow hair. Big and bold glitter decorates one side of her face and the tip of her tailfin.

She looks magical.

Dashing to her station, she calls for places backstage.

Everything is as ready as she and I can possibly make it. My work here is done.

I take a deep breath and swim to the offstage area where I'll have a good view of the show. I'm so glad I decided to come. Even though it meant seeing Zak. It was worth it.

When everyone is in position for the start of the show, Zanzia swims out of the wings and to the downstage center mark. She grins as she faces the crowd.

"Greetings, fellow Thalassinians," she says, her voice loud enough to command the attention of the entire auditorium and excited enough to set the crowd on the edge of their seats. "Welcome to the tenth annual Queen Sirenia Academy Give Back Week Cabaret."

She holds out her arms.

On that cue, a pair of stagehands shoot off glitter canons, sending silver, pink, and teal sparkles shimmering over the stage and swirling out into the audience.

"You are in for a treat tonight," Zanzie continues, "with the most talented group of performers to ever grace our stage."

The crowd cheers, and I can't help but applaud. She's worked so hard on this. Sure, Goby helped, but Zanzie was definitely the driving force.

I can't believe I almost missed this.

"But first," she says, and the crowd quiets down, "I'm going to give the stage over to my big brother. Zak?"

The crowd cheers again—when wouldn't they cheer for their favorite seaball star?—but I'm confused. Zanzia never mentioned to me that Zak had anything to do with the show.

And the idea that he is voluntarily choosing to speak in public? That's…surprising.

What do I know? Maybe his speech before the big game cured him of his fear. I should be proud of helping him overcome that. Instead, all I can focus on is the way my heart pounds violently in my throat from the second he swims out onto the stage.

I can't help but hold my breath as he floats into place.

Zak scans the crowd. Clears his throat. Glances offstage left, where Zanzia gives him an encouraging nod. Then he looks offstage right.

Directly at me.

He stares at me—hard—for like three solid seconds, before turning his attention back to the crowd.

"Most of you are probably expecting me to say something about seaball," he says, his voice steady and serious.

The crowd cheers in response. He waits a moment for them to quiet down.

"But what I have to say has nothing to do with sports," he tells them. "It has to do with feelings."

The crowd falls silent, some of them shifting uncomfortably in their seats.

Some idiot in the back shouts, "Stick to seaball!"

Zak smiles. "Sounds like I'm not the only one who needs to learn how to deal with his feelings like a grown-up."

146

He stares out at the silent auditorium for a second before continuing.

"Let me tell you a story," he says. "Once upon a time, there were two friends." His tailfin swishes back and forth nervously. "Or at least I thought they were just friends. One of them wanted more."

In an instant my face is on fire. Literal, burning like the sun, on fire.

Yeah, yeah, I know I'm underwater and how could you catch fire underwater, Coral? Well, I don't know. Science hasn't answered every question. Yet. But I can promise you that it just happened.

Any second now the entire ocean around me is going to vaporize.

Zak glances quickly at me—just in case I had any doubt as to who he's talking about—and then back at the crowd.

"For reasons I won't go into with you lovely group of strangers," he continues, "they decided to pretend to be something more for a little while."

If there were a way that the seafloor could open up and swallow me whole right now, I would one-thousand-percent sign up for that option. What part of no-one-can-ever-know-it's-fake did he not understand? All of it, apparently.

Now I know *why* my face is on fire. It's so I can burn him alive as soon as he's off the stage. I must be channeling some sort of revenge goddess energy.

"And along the way—" He glances my way again, this time letting his gaze remain on me. "—the other friend started wanting more, too."

Someone lets out a startled squeak. It takes me a few seconds to realize that someone was me.

I can't have heard him right. There is no way he just said what I think he said. I must be having the hearing version of hallucinations. Because what I think I heard is that maybe Zak's feelings for me weren't as fake as I thought.

Sure, I'd hoped for that. But could it actually be true?

I'm frozen in place. This can't be happening.

"But by that point," he continues, eyes still trained on me, "things had gotten so complicated that neither one of them knew how to turn the fake thing into a real thing."

My jaw could not drop any lower if I was an actual anglerfish. I half expect some unsuspecting little perch to swim on in.

The idiot in the back of the auditorium shouts, "Get to the point!"

"The point," Zak says, finally returning his attention to the crowd, "is that when your feelings for someone change, you should let them know."

I brace myself for the idiot to make a snarky comeback. Zak must be waiting for the same thing because he pauses. When the retort doesn't come, Zak pushes on.

"When you realize that you love someone, you shouldn't let a single second go by without telling them."

He floats there, awkwardly, staring out at the crowd. Eyes straight ahead. Decidedly *not* looking at me.

While I can't stop staring at him.

My brain has stopped working properly. It's started thinking—no, *believing*—that my dreams have become reality. I've worked so hard for so long to keep the two separate.

Dreams are dreams. Reality is reality. Never the twain shall meet.

Maybe my brain is exhausted by the effort and has given up entirely. I wouldn't be surprised. I've put it through a lot in the last few days.

I study Zak, waiting for some clue. A hint that will tell me if I'm losing my mind, or if he's actually saying what I hope he's saying.

Nothing.

Zak floats there in the center of the stage. Staring straight ahead. Not moving, not saying anything.

The teeny-tiny part of my brain that isn't frozen in shock is impressed by how well he is handling his stage fright. I haven't seen a single tremble.

It feels like the entire theatre is holding its breath. Like the ocean has been sucked out of the space, and we're just waiting for the wave to crash back in with life-sustaining water.

Finally, the silence breaks. Someone in the crowd starts clapping. Then another someone. And another and another, until the entire audience is floating above their seats, applauding.

"Tell her," the idiot shouts. "Tell her now!"

Zak grins as he turns to face me.

I have never blinked so many times so fast in all my life. This can't possibly be happening. This must be a delusion. A total break with reality.

Because the worst part is…I want it to be true. I *need* it to be true.

And if it's not…. I don't know how my heart can survive a break like that.

I start floating back, away from the stage. I bump into something—some*one*—Chromis.

"S-sorry," I stammer.

I'd completely forgotten that I asked him to meet me here.

Chromis gives me a wry smile. "I believe my services as a backup date are no longer necessary."

I nod and shake my head at the same time. I can barely make sense of his words, let alone offer any sort of coherent response.

Zanzia returns to the center of the stage, preparing to start the show for real.

Zak kicks off in my direction.

For reasons that will probably never make sense, I turn and swim away.

SEVENTEEN

Saturday evening, even later

I MAKE it out of the theatre and around the back before
Zak catches up with me.

"Coral, wait."

I freeze. I can't think. I can barely breathe.

What he said in there—in front of everyone—can't be
true. Can it?

"Please," he says, "talk to me."

Words won't come out, so I just laugh.

"Okay…" He flashes me that patented Zak Marlin grin.
"I'll talk."

He kicks himself a little closer. Part of me wants to close
the distance more. Part of me wants to put even more space
between us.

In the end, I split the difference and stay where I'm at.

Zak's grin turns into something softer, something I've

never seen before. Looks like I'm going to have to add a #11 spot to my list.

"I'm sorry I couldn't figure out a way to say it sooner. Or, you know—" He gestures back toward the theater. "—in front of fewer people."

I can't believe he did that. But on the list of things I can't believe right now, that's nowhere near the top.

"But I'm not sorry that it happened that way. I'm glad all of those people know how I feel about you." His gaze drops and his lashes lower, making him look like a shy little merboy. "I want everyone to know."

I've never seen Zak timid before. This is something new. Something different.

I want to respond. I know I should. It's just not really possible at the moment.

"What— But—" I shake my head hard, trying to get my words to form an actual sentence. All I can manage is, "How?"

"How?" he repeats with a gentle laugh. "Does it matter?"

I can only move my head in a weird mix of yes and no signals. It doesn't matter, but it also does.

Yeah, it doesn't make sense to me, either.

"I can barely remember what the ocean was like before you were part of my life," he says. "I've always loved you."

My breath catches in my throat.

"Now I just love you in a different way." He reaches out, like he wants to touch me, but then drops his hand back to his side.

My eyes sting with tears.

This can't be happening. This can't be my life, my reality. I've wanted this for so long, I'm afraid that it's some kind of horrible joke.

The Zak I know would never, ever be that cruel. But my heart is still battered and broken and not ready to trust.

Zak swims closer, until only inches separate us. He reaches up and brushes my cheek with his fingertips.

"Don't cry, Coral. Please don't—"

Before I can stop myself, I close the distance between us and press my hand over his mouth and my lips to my hand.

It's the closest thing to a kiss without igniting the magical bond between us. If that's destined to happen, there will be a perfect time for it in the future. But for now, right now, I need the reassurance of that connection.

My body fills with energy, sparkling and dancing like glitter floating down through sunlit water. His hands come up to cup my face. Like he's savoring this precious moment as much as I am.

I mirror his movements, pressing my free palm to his jaw, as if I'm trying to memorize every single sensation. His palms against my cheeks. His lips against my palm. Heat and electricity everywhere.

Then reality resurfaces. In a flash, the moment is over. I kick back, press my hands to his shoulders and shove him away.

"What about Angel?" I demand.

He looks so adorably confused that I want to take back what I said and get back to not-kissing him. But I know I can't. I'm so confused right now. I need answers.

"This—" I gesture between us. "It was about getting

Angel back. And it worked. You're back together." My throat burns sour as I say, "You got what you wanted."

I might throw up. I mean, I haven't eaten anything since yesterday, but it's still possible.

I'm a moron.

Why did I have to bring up Angel? Why did I have to ruin what was most definitely the most perfect moment of my entire life? Why couldn't I just live in that fantasy for as long as possible?

Instead, I pulled out a pin and popped the bubble.

I'm bracing myself for the realization to dawn on Zak— and the subsequent lifetime of regret—when he shakes his head.

"I never wanted that."

"But—"

"Coral, *I* broke up with *her*."

My jaw drops for like the millionth time today. "What?"

He smiles and gently takes my hands off his shoulders so he can lace our fingers together. I can't decide whether to stare at our hands or at his face. Rather than make myself dizzy looking back and forth, I focus my eyes on his.

"We told everyone she dumped me so she could save face." He gives me an embarrassed smile. "We're still friends, and I didn't want to make it harder on her than it had to be."

My brain struggles to connect the dots. Zak broke up with Angel? I mean, duh, that makes way more sense than the idea that Angel dumped him. Only a fool would end things with Zak Marlin, and Angel is no fool.

"But that's why you wanted this fake relationship," I argue.

I try to make that same between-us gesture but forgot that Zak is holding my hand, so I actually end up pulling us closer together.

"*I* wanted to get my mom off my back," he argues. "*You* were the one who said it would help me get Angel back."

"I did?"

"You did." He smiles. "Without even asking me if that's what I wanted."

I replay as much of that conversation as I can recall. I was still in shock about the whole idea, so parts are definitely a blur. But I remember the general gist.

Son of a swordfish, he's right. I'm the one who brought Angel into it.

But that doesn't explain what happened yesterday.

"After the game," I say, "you were hugging."

Zak slowly rubs his thumb across the back of my hand. I try to maintain focus on the conversation, but it's getting harder and harder the more he touches me.

"Being away at college is what made me realize how wrong Angel and I were together." He turns my hand over and continues the motion against my palm. "Seeing me happy with you is what made her realize it too."

"It did?"

I'm getting a little dizzy. Or maybe this is just what giddy happiness feels like.

"She came up to me after the game to tell me she's happy for me." He shrugs. "She's happy for us."

I take a deep, shaky breath as it all starts to fall into place.

"But that—?"

He nods. "Mmm-hmm."

"And you—?"

He shakes his head. "Nope."

"So we—?"

"Now you're getting the idea."

I stare at him, so totally and utterly confused, but also seeing with a clarity that my crush-blind heart never let me have. That look on his face? I've seen it in my dreams since the day we met.

The fact that it's now a part of my reality is just mind-boggling. Is it even physically possible to be this happy?

Zak floats closer and presses his forehead against mine.

"It stopped being fake for me days ago," he whispers.

I can't help but whisper back, "When?"

He grins. "When you didn't puke on our third Torpedo Whirl ride."

I laugh. A complete and utter full-body laugh. The happiness glitter that's sparkling through my body just explodes out in one huge burst of joy.

"And," he says, his voice taking on a more serious tone, "when you helped me get through my game day speech."

"I would do that for anyone."

"Exactly." He squeezes my hand. "And when you showed up to help your best friend, even after you thought her brother broke your heart."

A wave of guilt washes over me. "I almost didn't."

"But you did." He pulls me closer. "You are a uniquely amazing mergirl, Coral Ballenato."

"Then no wonder we're such a good match." I wrap my arms around his neck. "Because you are a uniquely amazing merguy, Zak Marlin."

"Just imagine how uniquely amazing we'll be together."

"Oh, I have," I tell him. "I have."

Then he presses his palm to my lips and not-kisses me, and I don't have to imagine anymore. Reality is so much better than I ever dreamed.

Dear reader,

While writing *Pretty in Pearls*, I knew instantly that Riatus's little sister wanted a story of her own. She was spunky and quirky and a total romantic.

I hope you loved reading about her and her seaball star as much as I loved writing about them. If you did, please share your love by leaving a review.

To get breaking news, exclusive giveaways, and early access to new stories, visit teralynnchilds.com/subscribe to join my mailing list.

My dive into the mermaid world is far from over. I have more stories to tell, in Thalassinia and beyond. Flip the page to find out how you can help....

Tera L. Childs

NEXT IN THIS SERIES

Want even more books in the Forgive My Fins world? Is there a particular character whose story you desperately want to read? Help TLC pick who to write about next by voting at teralynnchilds.com/poll-wcw.

Follow TLC on one of these sites to get notified when the new release is available.

amazon.com/author/tlc

bookbub.com/profile/tera-lynn-childs

goodreads.com/teralynnchilds

THANK YOUS

A huge shout out to my Mythfit beta readers, who helped me polish and perfect this story—and saved me from one especially huge potential plot disaster! This book wouldn't be possible without the hard work and keen eyes of Camden, Deborah, Rachel, and Reilly.

Thank you!!!

ABOUT THE AUTHOR

TERA LYNN CHILDS (*Authora sirena*) is species of authorfish that always dreamed of being a mermaid, but never got closer than a career as a competitive swimmer. Loves to spend as much time as possible in and around water, right up until her fingertips turn all pruney, in the vain hope that one day her legs will magically turn into fins. When stuck on land, you can find *Authora sirena* writing in coffee shops across the country, prowling for cool mermaid gear on Etsy, and creating worlds of myths, mermaids, and magic in her books for teens and other awesome people. Find her online at *teralynnchilds.com*.

MORE BY TLC

the Oh. My. Gods. series

Oh. My. Gods.

Goddess Boot Camp

Goddess in Time

the Forgive My Fins series

Forgive My Fins

Fins Are Forever

Just For Fins

Pretty in Pearls

the Sweet Venom trilogy

Sweet Venom

Sweet Shadows

Sweet Legacy

the Darkly Fae series

THE MORAINE CYCLE

When Magic Sleeps

When Magic Dares

When Magic Burns

When Magic Falls

When Magic Wakes

Darkly Fae: The Moraine Cycle

Myths and Mistletoe

the City Chicks series

Eye Candy

Straight Stalk

Trying Texas

City Chicks: Volume 1

CPSIA information can be obtained
at www.ICGtesting.com
Printed in the USA
LVHW111540040720
659747LV00007B/121/J